DOUBLE HELIX

Nancy Werlin

DIAL BOOKS | NEW YORK

Published by Dial Books
A member of Penguin Group (USA) Inc.
345 Hudson Street
New York, New York 10014

LIBRARY OF CONGRESS CATALOGING-IN-PUBLICATION DATA

Werlin, Nancy.
    Double helix / Nancy Werlin.
        p.   cm.
Summary: Eighteen-year-old Eli discovers a shocking secret about his life and his
family while working for a Nobel Prize–winning scientist whose specialty is genetic
engineering.
    ISBN 0-8037-2606-6
    [1. Genetic engineering—Fiction. 2. Bioethics—Fiction. 3. Huntington's
chorea—Fiction. 4. Science fiction.] I. Title.
    PZ7.W4713Do   2004
    [Fic]—dc22   2003012269

Designed by Kimi Weart
Text set in Galliard

Printed in the U.S.A. on acid-free paper

10 9 8 7 6 5 4 3 2 1

For my father, Arnold Werlin,
a quiet hero

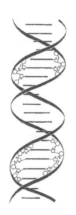

CHAPTER 1

IT WAS ALMOST IMPOSSIBLE for me to sit still—but I had to. I couldn't be pacing frantically back and forth across the rich gray carpet of Wyatt Transgenics's expansive reception area when Dr. Wyatt—*the* Dr. Wyatt—

But he'd send an assistant to get me, wouldn't he? To escort me to his office? He wouldn't come himself.

My knuckles were tapping out a random jumpy rhythm on the arm of the chair. I clenched my fist to stop it. I shifted my legs.

The chair I sat in was small and hard and low to the ground. Obviously, whoever designed the corporate reception area had been focused not on the comfort of visitors, but on showcasing the enormous double-helix staircase that dominated the atrium with its depiction of DNA structure. And though anyone would find the chairs uncomfortable, they were particularly bad for me. My knees stuck up awkwardly, making the pant legs of my borrowed suit look even shorter than they were. There was nothing I could do about that—my father was only six foot three. His jacket, also, was too tight across the shoulders on me.

I tugged at my tie. I suspected—no, I knew I looked ridiculous. The suit didn't even make me look older. And I now thought it had been completely unnecessary. In the time I'd been sitting here, at least a dozen Wyatt Transgenics employees had moved purposefully across the mezzanine area at the top of the double-helix staircase, and they'd all been wearing casual clothes. Sneakers. Jeans. T-shirts under lab coats. The only people in suits were the two security guards.

I could hear Viv's voice in my ear. Philosophical. *Well, who knew? We both thought you ought to wear a suit.*

We had. Viv had at first tried to convince me to buy a suit in the right size from a store. She'd been appalled when I explained the cost of a man's suit, and, undeterred, had spent all yesterday afternoon dragging me through used clothing stores in Cambridgeport. *Excuse me, but do you have any suits that would fit my boyfriend?*

When she'd failed to find one, she'd burst into tears. Right in the middle of Central Square.

Viv. If she weren't in my life . . . well. I couldn't imagine how lonely I would be.

Guilt stirred in me, though. Viv thought this was a job interview of some kind. A summer internship. I hadn't lied to her. I never lied to Viv. I had just, as always, kept quiet and let her think whatever she chose.

Of course, I could have kept it a secret that I was coming.

But I'd felt as if I would burst if I couldn't say something. And who was there but Viv to confide in, even a little? I wasn't going to tell my father.

Once more I caught myself fidgeting, looking at the clock. My appointment had been for twenty minutes ago. I'd checked in with the receptionist ten minutes early, so I'd been here half an hour. I tried to work up irritation at being kept waiting. Dr. Wyatt was a busy man, an important man, a Nobel Prize winner, probably one of the most important scientists alive today—but it was he who'd invited me. He who'd set the date and time. I'd had to duck out of school an hour early to get here by bus. It was rude of him to keep me waiting so long.

But the truth was, I didn't care. I was consumed by curiosity . . . and anxiety. I'd wait all afternoon if I had to.

Bottom line: I had no idea why I was here. Why I'd been . . . summoned. The woman who called me had simply said: *We got your email. Dr. Wyatt has read it. He would like to meet you.*

She did not say it was a job interview. She had not asked me to send, or bring, a résumé or a school transcript or any teacher recommendations.

We got your email.

I had emailed Dr. Wyatt. I had found his address on the Wyatt Transgenics website and I had written to him. That was a fact. Three weeks ago. But it had been a big mistake, a drunken impulse that had embarrassed me seconds after I'd clicked Send, and certainly it had never occurred to me that Dr. Wyatt himself would read my message. It was inconceivable that it had caused an invitation—no, my earlier word was more accurate: a summons.

A command?

What was I doing here? Was this truly a job interview with Quincy Wyatt himself?

"Eli Samuels?" The voice from the mezzanine level was pitched normally, but it carried down to me as clearly as if the speaker were using a microphone.

My head jerked up. I found myself scrambling out of my chair. Staring up.

And . . . there he was. Dr. Quincy Wyatt, the man himself, twenty feet above me, standing at the top of the spiral of the double helix. He looked exactly like he did in the photographs. That big head with the tight, grizzled, reddish-white hair. The round black-rimmed glasses. The steel cane clenched in his left hand.

Viv's voice again. *He's a legend, Eli! I mean, from seventh-grade biology class—Gregor Mendel, Watson and Crick, Quincy Wyatt. We had to learn all that stuff, remember?*

I remembered, all right. I remembered, for reasons I'd never told Viv—and never would, either.

I stared up the stairs at him. He at least was wearing a suit—a cream-colored linen suit, with a beige shirt. His fit him better than mine did me. I was suddenly very conscious of my ankles, sock-clad but otherwise exposed to the world in the gap between the hem of my father's pants and my shoes.

Then Dr. Quincy Wyatt lifted one hand and beckoned. And, though I made no conscious decision to move, I found myself walking.

I crossed the reception area. I mounted the stairs. I felt his gaze on me, piercing, bright, interested. And when I reached the mezzanine, I stood quite still—it didn't even occur to me to put out my hand in an offer to shake—and he examined my face for two full minutes. I stood patient as a statue as his eyes took me in, missing—I knew—nothing. Not the ill-fitting suit, not the bulge of the book in my pocket, not the backpack dangling from my hand. Not even—I'd have sworn—a grain of my skin.

The most acute mind on the planet, he'd been called.

I wondered if he could see my soul. My lies to Viv. The drunken disaster I'd been that endless horrible spring night, after it had become clear to my father that no college acceptances or even rejections had arrived, and I told him the truth: They would not, because I had applied nowhere.

I thought that maybe I wouldn't mind if Dr. Wyatt could see everything.

At last, he nodded. "Eli Samuels," he said again. There was a tone to his voice—as if I were a specimen now satisfactorily labeled and classified—that reinforced my idea that he understood me better, somehow, than anyone else ever had, or would.

"Hello, Dr. Wyatt," I said. The words came out a little croaked; I had to clear my throat. And then I heard myself add inanely: "Here I am." I wanted to disappear; I felt so stupid.

But: "Indeed, Eli Samuels," said Dr. Wyatt. "Here you are."

Then he smiled directly at me. He smiled the way Viv's mother does when I come home with Viv after school. The smile caused his cheeks to lift into little mountains on his face. And somehow I knew that I didn't need to be nervous or afraid anymore.

I smiled back. I was too relieved to do it well.

Dr. Wyatt lifted his steel cane a fraction of an inch from the floor, just enough to gesture with it. "Come with me into my office," he said, and turned. He limped a little as he moved, but he used the cane deftly, and I followed him in the same way that, as a child, I'd toddled confidently after my mother.

CHAPTER 2

DR. WYATT'S OFFICE WAS NOT what I would have expected. First, the placard beside the door said only: Quincy Wyatt. No "President," no "Chief Scientist"—no simple "PhD," even. Then we stepped inside, and I felt my eyebrows literally lift with surprise.

The room was the size of a large closet. It had no windows. Two cheap folding tables were set against the walls, the right-hand one heaped with teetering stacks of papers, journals, and magazines. The stacks covered the entire surface except a dusty little clearing around a framed photograph of a gorgeous catamaran. The left-hand table held a computer monitor and keyboard, two opened bottles of root beer—both half full—and a large canister of Tinkertoys with a few sticks and spools scattered out on the table. The single chair was a standard office swivel, but with a dangerously jagged piece of metal where one of its arms ought to be.

"We'll need another chair," said Dr. Wyatt. I wanted to offer to get it—he used a cane to walk, after all—but I didn't know where to go, and I didn't want to offend him, and anyway he was back again in an instant, wheeling a maroon chair that looked considerably more comfortable than the one already in his office. It also possessed both arms. He pushed this chair in my direction and I caught it.

"Sit down, young Eli," he said. His tone was one of command—I thought of how he'd beckoned me up the double-helix staircase a few minutes ago—and I felt a moment of reflexive rebellion. But after I'd maneuvered the chair into the office between the folding tables, I did sit.

After all, no one had forced me to keep this appointment. I had come of my own free will, come in this silly suit and tie, because I wanted—hoped—

I contained myself.

Dr. Wyatt closed the door and moved his chair directly in front of it before sitting down himself. Then he looked at me, and I looked back at him—the large head, the squat body in the expensive linen suit—and felt shame and anxiety descend fully upon me again.

The email I'd sent to him—a man I didn't even know. The begging undertone. I hadn't been able to bear to think of it, but now—

Okay, wait. I had options. I could take control of this situation immediately. Get the embarrassment over up front. I could almost hear myself speaking.

Dr. Wyatt, about that email. Let me just say that I've been under some stress. Family stuff. My mom is—I searched for a good, neutral word—*sick nowadays, but when I was a kid, she mentioned you . . . and I got drunk one night—just that once, my father and I had just had a fight about something—plus I'd found this stupid letter that made me angry at him, and the letter mentioned you . . . and I've always been interested in biology . . . and I'm putting off college . . . and anyway, I wrote that email asking for a job. It was an impulse and a bad one. I'd like to apologize. I know it was out of line.*

Would that work? Or would all the half-truths and evasions be obvious? Viv I could deceive—she loved me, she was willing to be deaf, dumb, and blind when I needed her that way—but a stranger, a scientist . . . Or maybe it would be better if I waited to hear what he had to say first. Maybe that would actually give me more control.

Sometimes—no, often—I hated being a teenager. Hated not having the full control I wanted. Even by the time you're eighteen, adults don't take you seriously. Even at eighteen, you're considered a kid.

All these thoughts flashed through my head in seconds, but I could feel Dr. Wyatt watching me the whole time, and it was uncomfortable. I felt a bead of sweat form on my forehead near my hairline, and I prayed it wouldn't trickle embarrassingly down. The tiny airless office, this narrow chair, my borrowed suit—I felt trapped.

Why didn't he say something? Was it to force me to speak first? I wouldn't.

And this chair was too short.

Well, to hell with that. My hands reached beneath the office chair and located the knobs to adjust it. I pressed and prodded, and miraculously the chair shot up to its full height. My knees shifted from chest level to a more normal position. Suddenly I could breathe more easily, and the panic receded.

"Better?" said Dr. Wyatt conversationally.

I nodded.

He leaned forward. "I'm wondering, Eli: How tall are you exactly?"

Now this was a conversation I had practically every day, and was quite comfortable with. "I'm six foot seven."

"And you're only what—eighteen?"

"Yes."

"What does your doctor say about your final height?"

I shrugged as if I didn't know. But the truth was that I didn't like to say because people make too much of it. And maybe because my mother used to do imitations of Dr. Kaplan for her friends. *Get ready, Mr. and Mrs. Samuels, he's headed for seven feet. But with a little luck there'll be college basketball scholarships, which will more than compensate for the clothing and shoe bills.*

Dr. Wyatt was squinting at me. "Six eleven," he muttered. "But not seven feet."

I felt shock at his near-accuracy. He barreled on like some long-lost uncle: "How about school? You're about to graduate here in Cambridge? It would be public school, right? Rindge and Latin High?"

"Yes." Hope surged in me. He was acting like this really was some kind of job interview.

"How'd you do? All A's? Are you the valedictorian, Eli?"

"No." I felt a secret spurt of satisfaction.

"Salutatorian, then?"

I was astonished. "Uh, yeah . . ."

"Well, don't tell me you couldn't have been valedictorian if you wanted. You held back—why? Do you have some guilt at having done well in the genetic lottery?"

I blinked. What a very strange way to put it—and how had he guessed that I had, in fact, held myself back?

Viv was to be class valedictorian. She was thrilled. And as for me, well, anything Viv wanted, assuming it was in my power to give, she would get. Even if, as in this case, she couldn't know I had given it. It was one of my secret rules to help things go well with us.

"That's my own business," I said.

Dr. Wyatt reached across the table for the Tinkertoy canister. He dumped some of its contents out and said, "Well, whatever your reasoning, it was a foolish move. You shouldn't let any award or recognition slip away, particularly not out of some misplaced delicacy about others' feelings. Awards can be useful to you. And people simply accept, though they don't necessarily like, the plain fact that intellectual resources are distributed unequally." He shrugged. "That's life, Eli."

I didn't know what to say.

Dr. Wyatt picked up a red Tinkertoy stick and fitted it into the central hole of a wooden spool. He placed the spool flat on the table, with the spoke sticking up, and regarded it. Without looking up, he continued: "What are your college plans?"

"I'm taking a year off. Then I'll go to college."

He had attached a second wooden spool to the top of the red stick. "Where will you go?"

Viv was going to Brandeis. Very near. "I don't know yet. I'll apply this year."

Dr. Wyatt scowled. "You have to go to college. Biggest mistake of your life not to. You should go to a good one, too."

I could have mentioned Bill Gates and other wildly successful non-graduates, but why bother? "I know," I said calmly. "I do plan to go."

"And this year off? You'll do what with it? Travel?"

"No." I was going to visit my mom as often as I could stand to, and see lots of Viv; that was all I knew for sure. "I need to get a job. I was actually hoping that—" I took a deep breath. "I'd like to work here. If . . . if that's possible."

"Ah." Dr. Wyatt had made a double-wheel kind of structure with the Tinkertoys. The spoke was green. The structure seemed to have his total attention. "You got A's in chemistry and biology?"

"And physics."

A pause. Then, calmly, easily: "All right, then. You can work here for the year. It will look great on your college applications. You'll like the work—it'll be low-level, but you'll see interesting things. And I'll enjoy having you around. We can talk from time to time."

This was what I wanted. But still, my mouth dropped open with shock. And I thought, maybe, maybe if I worked here, if I talked to Dr. Wyatt from time to time, I could find some way to ask—to find out—

"Well?" Dr. Wyatt prompted. "Would you like that, Eli? It's not every kid who has the opportunity to work at Wyatt Transgenics. Most of our employees—even the lab workers—have master's degrees. Doctorates."

"I would like it," I said. It was true. Everything else aside—my God! Wyatt Transgenics!

"Then that's settled." Dr. Wyatt pushed the finished Tinkertoy structure away and stood up. "Let's get you down to Human Resources. We can probably pay you something nice."

"But—"

"What?"

"But why would you want to hire me?"

Another pause.

Then: "I knew your mother," said Dr. Wyatt. "Years ago." And now he was, indeed, looking at me straight on. "I knew both your parents, but especially your mother. Ava Samuels. Nice woman. I knew she'd had a son named Eli, so I knew who you must be immediately, when I got your message. So of course I'd like to do your parents' son a favor.

"But we won't talk about your parents, Eli. Your mother. There is no need to. We both understand the situation, eh?"

I stared at him. His linen suit. His big head. His eyes, mere pinpricks behind the black-framed glasses. Slowly his words sank in, and as they did, I felt something. I felt relief, and comfort, and security, of a kind that I hadn't experienced—except maybe when I held Viv close—for years.

Even if I didn't understand what he meant by "the situation."

"Do you want a job, then?" said Dr. Quincy Wyatt. *The* Dr. Quincy Wyatt. "Is it a deal?" He stuck out his hand, as he had not done less than an hour ago when we met.

I did not hesitate. I put my hand in his, and we shook, firmly.

CHAPTER 3

OUTSIDE THE IMPOSING MODERN brick-and-glass cathedral that was Wyatt Transgenics, it was a perfect May afternoon. I decided to walk the three miles home, following the pedestrian path along the Charles River until I could turn off onto Western Avenue and up into deepest Cambridgeport.

I was so filled with incredulous exuberance that I wished I could run. But even though I'd taken off the jacket, the fact that I was wearing my father's suit made running a bad idea. I stuffed the tie in my backpack and walked fast instead.

I was going to be a lab assistant at Wyatt Transgenics, starting the Monday after graduation. That was in two weeks. Unbelievable. Unbelievable! I couldn't have planned it even if I'd tried . . . or anyway, not so perfectly. It was a form of adulthood, sooner than I'd dared hope for. Adulthood—and control. Power over my own destiny.

Viv would keel over with happiness when I called her. What a bonus for me that was. It had worried her so much that I wasn't planning for college next year. *It's just not like you,* she'd said mournfully.

I made a little bet with myself now. When I told her about the job offer, and my acceptance, Viv would say solemnly, *We should always trust the universe, Eli. I should have known better than to doubt.*

Viv and her trustworthy universe. I grinned and shook my head. I could never understand how it was that Viv could genuinely believe all would be for the best in the end. It wasn't like she was the kind of fool who went around thinking everything was always wonderful. I'd known that about her ever since that one day back in fifth grade, when we were both eleven.

I'd entered the boys' room ten minutes before Scott Eisenstadt, Jake Fitzhugh, and Mike Wynne were due—the news was all over school—to drag Asa Barnes in so they could beat the crap out of him and hold his head in the toilet and . . . well, who knows. I was big and strong even then, and I had every intention of stopping this nastiness toward Asa for good. But there would be an unholy mess of denials and counter-accusations and lies and suspensions and parental interference ahead, and I was not looking forward to it. I just didn't see another way.

Viv did, though. I found she had occupied the boys' room ahead of me. She was standing on a toilet, artfully hidden by the stall's carefully ajar door, with a scared but grim look on her face and a video camera in her hands.

We each knew instantly what the other was doing. It was the

first time I saw how beautiful Vivian Fadiman is when she smiles directly at you.

She lifted her camera slightly, her brows quirking in a question.

I said, "New plan. I'll go back out, and after they get here, I'll give you exactly a minute and a half to get some good footage. Make sure you get sound, too. *Then* I'll interrupt. And if you need me here earlier, scream and I'll come."

She nodded. The rescue mission—our rescue mission—proceeded exactly as if we were undercover agents who'd worked together forever. And even though we didn't become friends then, there was always my knowledge that Viv was . . . well, was the girl who'd figured out how to save Asa Barnes from hell, and then did it.

Maybe, I thought now, that long-ago incident was one reason why Viv believed things always ended well. Maybe, for her, the universe had always proved trustworthy.

If that was the case, then I hoped she would never know the truth.

I crossed Memorial Drive, heading away from the river, now only a few blocks from home. I decided that as soon as I got my first paycheck, I would take Viv to the most elegant restaurant in Boston. And I would buy flowers for my mother's room at the nursing home. She loved—had loved—irises, yellow roses, and some other flowers I didn't know the names of but might recognize at the florist's. I would order a new arrangement to be delivered every week.

I could afford it. They were going to pay me $18 an hour.

That turned into about $2,000 a month, after taxes and deductions.

When I compared it with my current after-school minimum-wage job running backups for a local computer company, it seemed a dizzying fortune. I could help out with the bills—I'd force my father to let me help. And maybe there'd be money left over. Maybe—

I indulged in fantasies about renting an apartment of my own. I never had and never would bring Viv to the apartment I shared with my father. And while Viv's mother was great—never knocked or came into Viv's room when we were in there with the door closed—well, it would be better to have a private place of our own. Obviously.

On the corner of my street, I stopped in a neighborhood grocerette, bought ramen noodles, apples, cereal, eggs, milk, barbecued corn nuts, and the local paper, and scanned the newspaper's rental listings right there in the grocery. That put a firm end to the apartment fantasy. I'd known before, anyway, because of what my father paid each month for our tiny two-bedroom. Even a studio apartment would eat up more than half my salary . . . and there were more important things to spend the money on, and ways to arrange it myself, too, if my father was a stiff-necked bastard about my giving him money directly.

Which he would be.

Inside our small brick building, I grabbed the mail and took the stairs two at a time to the fourth floor. I let myself into the apartment, which, after three years, still retained the unmistakably empty feel of the temporary.

My father was not there. Sometimes he went to the nursing home after work. Other times I didn't know what he did.

I changed out of the suit and wondered if I ought to take it to the dry cleaner's. I put on a pot of water for the ramen noodles. I was still fantasizing about the money. Maybe I could buy a car. That would help a lot next year because Viv's college was an hour away by public transportation, but only twenty minutes by car.

A car . . .

I had a thick folder in my backpack describing all the Wyatt Transgenics employment benefits. They ranged from the trivial to the terrifying, from discounted movie tickets to death and disability insurance. I thought I remembered something in there about a credit union that gave loans for used cars. I hauled the folder out and flipped it open.

Confidential counseling support in times of personal and family difficulties—I dropped that brochure as if it were printed in fire. Stock option purchase plan. Tax-sheltered retirement investments.

I couldn't find the credit union information, but I found myself frowning at the thick folder that contained all the details about the health insurance plan. There'd been an odd little scene at Wyatt Transgenics, after Dr. Wyatt had left me with the Human Resources director. The scene had involved health insurance . . . at first.

I had tried to tell the HR director, Judith Ryan, that I didn't need to sign up for the health plan. That I was never sick. But apparently this was one thing about which there was little choice. You could only get out of it if you were covered by some other plan.

"You need health insurance," Judith Ryan said. She had the whitest hands I'd ever seen. There was a heavy crystal bowl of hard candies on her desk and, on the wall behind her head, a poster of an owl accompanied by the words: *If you attend to the details, the details will attend to you.*

"After all, things happen. Let's suppose you're right, and you never get sick." Her voice told me she thought I was an idiot. "You could always get hit by a car."

She was indisputably right. But that didn't make me like her. However, it floated into my mind that I already had health insurance through my father's coverage. Surely it would be cheaper for my father if I took this on for myself?

I said, "You're right. I could get hit by a car. Or fall into an elevator shaft. Or, hey! Get infected by deadly microbes right in this building. You'd better sign me up."

"What did you just say?" I stared across the desk; Judith Ryan had drawn her body up fully in her seat, like a hooded cobra preparing to strike.

I was flummoxed. I searched my memory. "Sign me up?" I ventured.

"Before. That."

I thought she might haul off and hurl the crystal bowl of candy into my face. I was so unnerved that it actually took me a second to remember. Elevator shafts. Deadly microbes. "I was just joking."

"Wyatt Transgenics is a scientific laboratory. We do not joke about microbes and loose safety procedures."

Now I really was feeling like an idiot. "Okay," I said. I raised my hands in a placating gesture. "Okay. I get you. Sorry."

But she wasn't through. "We do not joke about these matters at work. We do not joke about these matters at home. We do not"—her glare grew more ferocious—"joke about them at school. Not to anyone. Not to friends, girlfriends, parents." Her nose squinched. "Not in messages written while inebriated."

She had read my email. Judith Ryan had read my embarrassing, begging email, which had literally begun with the words: *I wouldn't dare send this if I wasn't drunk.*

I hated her. But—I wanted this job.

"Okay," I said again. I had no clue what else I could say. "Okay. No jokes."

Perhaps a full half-minute elapsed, however, before Judith Ryan relaxed from the cobra position and resumed telling me—in a cool voice that had said it all many times before—about company benefits.

CHAPTER 4

I HEARD MY FATHER'S KEY in the lock and rapidly gathered together all the Wyatt Transgenics employment brochures and pieces of paper, stuffing them back into their folder.

"Hi," I called.

From the living room, my father gave a kind of grunt. Then, as if he had remembered that since the fight, we were being excruciatingly careful around each other—though we both knew the politeness was just the thin crust on a sleeping volcano—he called back: "Hello, Eli."

Calmly now, I slid the folder into my backpack and levered myself up from the kitchen table. It was only a few steps to the living room, where my father stood, facing away from me, riffling through today's mail.

His straight gray hair straggled nearly to the collar of his shirt. In a few days, I estimated, he'd go around the corner to the barber and emerge with a buzz cut that would do credit to an army sergeant. Then he'd ignore the matter for another year.

"How's school?" he said, his back still to me.

"Fine," I said.

"Still salutatorian?"

I almost didn't answer. "Yeah."

There was a slight pause, and then, as if our truce didn't exist, as if he couldn't help himself, my father bit out: "Not that it matters, since you're sending it all down the drain. You think I'm stupid? You don't fool me with your 'next year' story. If you're not careful, you'll ruin your life." He had still not turned to face me, and suddenly I longed more than anything to grab his shoulders, spin him around, and punch him hard, right in his stubborn face. His nose would crunch satisfyingly . . . it would bleed right onto his white shirt.

I took a deep breath. If I hadn't punched him on the night of the big fight, after reading that letter I'd found, I wasn't going to do it today.

The memory of Quincy Wyatt was oddly calming. Things were going to change from now on. I had a job, and a future that I had some sort of control over.

I wondered if my father had just come from visiting my mother at the nursing home, but I didn't ask. Nowadays we visited separately and didn't discuss her. "Anything interesting in the mail?" I said instead.

My voice came out evenly. He wasn't to know that, beneath the calm, I was remembering anew the letter that I'd discovered on the day we'd had the big fight. That short, formal letter that was, now, over ten years old. The letter that had prompted me to email Dr. Wyatt.

What had it been doing crumpled up at the back of the mail drawer in the hall table? Had my father tossed it in there on the day it arrived, when I'd been seven, and my mother had not yet begun to show symptoms? It was hard to believe that he'd leave such an important letter in the drawer as if it were a telephone bill or an old birthday card, and yet . . . he had. And, over time, the letter had worked its way to the back of the drawer, becoming one of several pieces of paper that for months had prevented the drawer from sliding in and out smoothly . . . until the day I'd finally gotten impatient enough to yank the whole drawer out and go fishing at the back for whatever was interfering.

The letter. I'd had to sit down after reading it. I'd been incredulous. Shocked. Scared. And then . . . I'd been angry.

I still was.

Every word was engraved in my memory.

Dear Mr. Jonathan Samuels:

This letter is to confirm in writing our telephone conversation of last Tuesday. As per Dr. Quincy Wyatt's request and referral, we have tested your blood sample and can confirm that you are negative for Huntington's disease. Congratulations.

However, we are aware that learning the results of one's HD test can be difficult even

when the news is good, as in this case. The
burden of years of anxiety is not so easily lifted,
and for many HD-Negatives, there are complex
additional family health concerns. Therefore, I
am enclosing information about counseling and
support groups. I urge you to investigate these.

If you have any further questions or need
assistance in any way, please call.

Sincerely,
Harriet Emerson, MSW
Genetics Counselor

I read the letter again in my mind as I stared at my father. He hadn't replied to my question, so I asked again. This time, my tone was a little testier. "I said, anything interesting in the mail?"

"Just bills." My father cut off his last word halfway through as he remembered that bills were another one of the rough points between us. It was, in fact, the only rough point that he knew about, because I hadn't mentioned the letter to him. Hadn't mentioned my secret rage.

My father must have been at risk for HD, too. It hadn't just been my mother. He must have been at risk, or why would he have taken the test?

His having been at risk didn't change my own risk profile, of course, since he was negative, according to the letter. So he couldn't have passed it on to me; only my mother could have done that. Still . . . how dare he not tell me?

But I had put the letter back. I had not wanted to talk about it, because, inevitably, he would then urge me again about my own testing. And I hadn't wanted to talk about it. Not now. Not yet. So, as far as he knew, we'd fought only about money that night. Money and college, which were the same thing, as far as I was concerned.

Not that money hadn't been enough to cause a fight between us. In fact, I felt my fists clench as I reminded myself of all the money problems he'd concealed from me these last few years, actually lying about the number of clients he had in his small private therapy practice, claiming to have raised his hourly rate, while he bleated to me about the importance of school and study and grades. But the fact was, long-term talk therapy with a psychologist like my father was out of fashion. It was expensive and time-consuming, and many health insurance plans didn't like to cover more than a half-dozen visits a year.

How had he thought we were going to pay for the expensive colleges he urged me to apply to? "Don't worry about it; we'll figure it out later," was not an answer.

I still didn't understand why he'd concealed our true financial circumstances from me. What was the point of concealment? He'd only have to tell me eventually, right? When would he have done that? After I was accepted at MIT or Stanford or Harvard? When I handed him the bill? Wouldn't that have been worse than telling me early enough so that I could try for scholarships, pick cheaper schools?

No, I didn't understand, but we weren't going to fight that

pointless battle again. I had changed the game—I now had the power and the control to do that.

"I got a job today," I said.

I saw his whole body jerk. He turned. His pale blue eyes fixed on my face. "What?"

"I got a job," I repeated. "I'm going to be a lab assistant. They're paying eighteen dollars an hour. I'll be giving you a lot of money toward the rent and food every month as soon as I get my first paycheck."

He was shaking his head in bewilderment, several steps behind me. "What? No! Wait, I—just where is this job, anyway?"

"Does it matter?" I asked. "Some company. What matters is that I mean it about the money. Don't try to tell me you don't need it. I want to contribute and I'm going to, and I'm going to do it my way. Oh, and—" A flashing image of Judith Ryan, in cobra posture, came to me, and I banished it. "—you can take me off your health insurance, the new job will cover it."

My father marched past me into the kitchen. I turned and watched his robotlike movements as he poured water into the coffee machine's reservoir, then spooned coffee into the filter.

"The college issue was already settled for next year," I said, after a few seconds. "You knew that."

He didn't look at me. "You could still take classes. Earn some credits to transfer later on." He pressed the Start button on the coffee machine. The machine hissed. A thin stream of coffee began to run down into the pot, and my father watched it with great attention.

I watched him.

"You're not being rational," I said to his profile. "I'll find a cheap way to do college in a year. I could have done that for next year if I'd known in time."

If he'd told me. If he'd been honest with me. Given me facts and figures and tax returns to send to colleges.

"We both know your mother wouldn't want—" he began.

And just like that, between one moment and the next, I lost control completely. "For all practical purposes, my mother is insane!" I yelled. "And who knows, maybe I—"

"Don't say it!" My father was yelling, too, all at once. "Stop saying that! You're fine!"

I did stop, mid-sentence. We both listened to the remembered sound of our screamed words in the little kitchen.

My father jerked the coffeepot out of the machine. A few stray drops of liquid dripped down onto the machine's warming plate and sizzled while my father tried to pour himself a cup. His hands were unsteady.

I reached for a single word, *Sorry,* and forced it out.

He nodded. The coffeepot shook visibly in his hand.

I walked to my bedroom and closed the door.

I sat down on the edge of my bed. I reached for my cell phone and held it in my hands.

A job? Eighteen dollars an hour? That's great! Tell me all about it, son. Tell me everything.

But it was okay. In a way, it was perfect, because I hadn't wanted to tell him where I'd be working. In fact, maybe I'd even provoked that little scene, guiding the conversation onto the rocks of anger, so I wouldn't have to tell him where, yet.

Maybe.

I could tell Viv, though. I would call her—surely she was home by now—and see if she wanted me to come over. She would, I knew. I could even stay there tonight.

And with her, I could pretend everything and everyone was normal.

CHAPTER 5

"Viv?" I kissed the top of her head and tightened my arms around her in silent apology for not letting her sleep. I'd told her all about the new job and she'd been as happy and excited as I'd expected. But now my mind was racing off in all sorts of odd directions instead of settling down.

She stirred, pressing back warmly. "Hmm?"

"I'm just wondering . . . I know it's been years since your father left, and you're used to it, but, well . . . you never talk much about him. Do you hate him?"

Viv didn't reply for so long that I wondered if she had fallen back to sleep, but then she moved forward, slightly away from me. "That's quite a question to ask at—" I felt her reach out to grab the little clock from her nightstand. "—12:03 in the morning. On a school night."

She shifted in bed to face me, and although there was no light, I imagined she could see my expression. The thought alarmed me. "Hey, I like holding you," I said, trying to maneuver her back into the spooning position.

But she wouldn't go. She propped herself up on one elbow and put the other hand against my chest. Her touch was gentle, but I knew that there was no chance this would be idle, intimate chat-before-sleep. Viv was in Serious Discussion Mode.

I tried to stop it. "We can talk about it another time. Or even not at all. I didn't mean to intrude."

"Oh, no intrusion. I guess it's true I've never talked about my father with you. I'm not sure why not." Even in the dark, I could still feel her staring as if she could see my face. "My father," she said, and then stopped.

I could actually feel the tightness spreading through her entire body. After a few moments, she made a noise as if she were trying to speak; and then her long hair brushed against my shoulders and chest as she moved her head from side to side. I reached with one hand to smooth her hair behind her.

I heard her draw a deep breath.

"Forget that!" she exclaimed. "*You* never talk about either of *your* parents! Never, Eli. Never!"

There was silence between us. I was in shock. I hadn't intended—

"Okay," I said rapidly. "Okay. I'm sorry. I get it. We have a deal, then. Forget it. You don't talk about your father, and I don't talk about my parents."

"No!" Viv said. More words came rushing out of her. "I don't have secrets from you, I'm happy to talk about my father sometime. But you . . ." She paused.

"What?" I noticed that I had somehow drawn away from her. There were inches more between us and the only point of contact was her hand.

"Eli, look. I didn't—I don't—want to pry. And I never meant to have this discussion now. But it was coming. You have to have known it was coming."

Uh, no. I had not.

"I'd never try to force you to talk about stuff you didn't want to talk about. But—but this has hurt me, okay? It's hurt me that you shut me out."

I didn't understand. How did my not talking about my parents hurt her in any way? But an apology was always a good thing to offer. "I'm sorry, Viv."

She kept right on talking. "It hurts me that you've never introduced me to your parents as your girlfriend—or even as your friend. You've never had me come over—and we've been going out for over a year. I've wondered if you were ashamed of me somehow. I mean, I know there are prettier girls than me . . . thinner girls—" She stopped abruptly.

I was filled with horror. "Viv." I couldn't think what to say. "No . . ."

"No?" she asked, and all the vulnerability in the world was in that one word.

I managed to reach out and pull her into me, and thankfully she came, and I held her tightly, her whole body against mine, skin to skin, warm. I stuttered. I said, "You have to know . . . Viv, you couldn't be more wrong . . ."

She was holding me tightly, too, now. Was she crying? I didn't know what to do. I held her.

Where had this come from? Could I fix it? Without—dear God, Viv couldn't meet my parents. Or even my father. It was simply not possible; the potential complications were too—complicated. There would be no way to ensure she wouldn't learn too much. Wouldn't be scared. Bottom line: I didn't want her to be part of all that. I didn't want her in that sad, frightening, depressing part of my life. I needed her in her nice separate compartment. I needed her to be an oasis. A safe, calm place for me.

I said to her, "I love you. There's nobody prettier. Nobody sexier. Plus, I hate really thin girls!" I cupped her hips. I thought for a second about groping for a condom packet and waving it above her nose in an attempt to make her laugh. But maybe she'd think I wasn't taking her seriously. "Come on. I'm telling you the truth. You're the one."

Finally I heard a muffled sort of agreeing noise. Slowly, she stopped shaking, and so did I. And then she gave a half-choke, half-laugh and lifted her head. I thought again about that condom—

"Actually," Viv said, "you know something? If we hadn't been going to school together all these years, if I didn't re-member meeting your parents back in grammar and middle school, I'd think you didn't have any parents at all."

"Oh," I said. "I do have them. Believe me."

"I know. It's just—I've had crazy thoughts, Eli, sometimes. That maybe they died, or they ran away. No one at school has seen them in years—they haven't come to parents' nights or college night or anything. I've wondered if maybe you're liv-ing all alone and you don't dare tell even me."

None of this was phrased as a question, but there was one there, nonetheless, and I wasn't going to be fool enough to ignore it. Or to try to divert her with sex.

"My parents are alive," I said carefully. "Both of them. I'm not living alone."

Viv rested her forehead on my chest again and her arms tightened. She whispered, "I love you so much. But this stuff . . ."

"I never meant to hurt you," I said.

"I know. But at least you understand now. I've been trying and trying to think of a way to tell you how I was feeling. I'm so glad I finally had the courage."

She was, too. I could tell. She thought everything would be okay now.

"Viv . . ." I said awkwardly. "I don't know if—we'll have to talk about this again, okay? Some other time? My parents—it's complicated. I don't know if you can meet them, and it's not anything to do with you."

She moved her head so that her cheek brushed my skin gently. "I figured it must be complicated. But what I'm asking—what I'm really asking for here is for you to trust me. Do you see that?"

I saw.

"I love you, Eli," she said earnestly. "And I believe you love me, but I need you to trust me. Even—especially—with the tough stuff. We have to have a relationship that's honest and open. There should be nothing we can't talk about."

I kissed her. What else could I do? "I love you very much, Viv Fadiman," I said. And, for now anyway, it satisfied her. In a little while, she actually slept.

I didn't.

CHAPTER 6

"I HAVE TO LEAVE NOW," I said politely to my father on the morning of graduation. I was aware that I sounded a little tense. "They're making us line up and rehearse marching a couple times before everybody gets there. I'll find you after the diplomas are handed out, okay?"

"All right," said my father, who was seated at the kitchen table. He looked at me over his bowl of cold cereal and I pretended to check something in my backpack. Cap. Gown. Disposable camera. Present for Viv.

Maybe I wouldn't find him afterward, I thought. Maybe instead I'd find somewhere to hide alone for a while. That might be the answer to the looming problem of Viv's expectations. If after half an hour he couldn't find me in the crowd, my father would probably walk home by himself from the ceremony. He might not even be surprised at my disappearance, with the way things had been between us.

I was vaguely aware that if I'd been somebody else, I might have been worried about delivering the five-minute speech I was supposed to give today. Viv was extremely nervous about her speech. But I wasn't. The speech was in my pocket. I'd read it. No big deal.

I was worried about afterward. Viv expected to meet my parents today. I hadn't had the guts to tell her that my mother wouldn't be coming or that I simply didn't want her to meet my father. Even though I could almost imagine performing a quick, formal introduction between them, I knew Viv wanted something else entirely. She wanted to have a real conversation, and if she got within three feet of my father, she would do her warm, friendly, intelligent best to make that happen. He'd respond, too, and then—and then, she would say something like, *I was looking forward to meeting Eli's mother, too. Where is she?*

My father was now raising an eyebrow at my shorts and T-shirt and sneakers.

"I'll be in the cap and gown anyway," I said. "No one will see these. And it's hot out."

Unexpectedly, he nodded. "I wore a tie-dyed shirt at my college graduation."

"Oh," I said. It was hard to remember that my father had once been a radical student type. But there were pictures of him and my mother to prove it. Somewhere.

My mind was really still on Viv. Maybe, if I was careful, this introduction could be done quickly and be over with. I said, casually, laying the groundwork: "There'll be kids dressed up and down, both. The valedictorian—that's Viv Fadiman—is dressing up. I'll probably introduce you to her later. She's a good friend of mine."

My father nodded absently. Then he frowned, and I had the sudden idea that he was trying to say something, but wasn't sure how to do it. He said finally, "Are you nervous about your speech?"

I felt a pang of guilt. To call my speech dull was to understate the case. It was a masterpiece of banality; I'd modeled it on a half-dozen of the dullest graduation speeches that I'd been able to find on the Internet. It had actually been pure cynical fun to write. And, of course, I was also making certain that if anybody did happen to talk about speeches afterward, it would be Viv's they praised. Until this moment, I hadn't thought much about how my father might feel as he listened to one unmemorable cliché after another.

"Uh," I said. "No. I'm not nervous."

"Really?"

"No. Viv Fadiman—the valedictorian, I just mentioned her—she's making the long speech. Mine is just a few minutes. No big deal."

"To me it is," said my father quietly. He looked me right in the face, and I realized then that this was what he'd been trying to say. That he—that despite all the anger between us lately—

And suddenly I felt like an experimental rat in a lab cage, with sharp objects jabbing at me from all sides. It was the emotional analogue to the way I'd felt yesterday, poked and prodded, tissue- and blood-sampled, lung-capacity and heart-rate measured, for nearly three hours in the medical exam that all new Wyatt Transgenics employees apparently had to undergo.

"Bye," I said abruptly. "See you later."

"See you later," said my father.

I ran, even though I wasn't eager to face Viv's expectations, either. But the day lay before me, and it had to be lived through. At least, I thought, I fully understood the situation. The afternoon would be like kayaking through white water. Terrible things might happen, sure, but you had studied the river's hazards, you trusted your instincts and your equipment, and you had survived tricky situations before.

In fact, as it actually said in my boring speech: *Be not troubled: for all things must pass.* Matthew, 24:6.

That was what I was thinking right up to the moment I stood behind the podium to deliver the speech. That was when I glanced casually out into the audience toward the eighth row of spectators, where I had seen my father sitting earlier—and found him standing. Standing, and staring, with incredulous fury pulsing off him—a fury that I could feel all the way from where I was.

I followed his eyes—

—to Dr. Quincy Wyatt, who was at that very moment using his cane to ease himself into an empty seat near the end of the second row.

Dr. Wyatt was oblivious to my father. But he seemed to feel my gaze. He looked right at me, caught my eye, and waved cheerfully. And I felt—rather than saw—my father witness this.

I hadn't told my father exactly where I was going to be working in my new job; so far, I'd avoided it as determinedly as I had avoided telling Viv too much about my parents. But I had told him enough. Lab assistant, I had said. And now, the omission spoke its own tale. I could see my father's comprehension . . . and his anger.

At some point after that—it probably wasn't any longer than twenty or thirty seconds—I became aware that people were waiting, were restive. I looked down at the printed pages of my speech. I opened my mouth and began reading. When I was done, I looked out at the audience for a few seconds, at my father, at Dr. Wyatt.

Then I sat down again, and Viv was squeezing my hand and whispering: "It was fine, Eli, really. You were just a little more nervous at the beginning than you'd expected."

I managed to squeeze her hand back and to clap loudly as she was called to the podium herself.

Be not troubled: for all things must pass.

Later on, much later, it occurred to me to check the context of that quote from Matthew. And then I had to laugh—if bitterly—because it didn't mean what I'd thought it did. Not for a second had it belonged in an ordinary graduation speech about good times past and ahead. Nor was it comforting.

See that ye be not troubled: for all these things must come to pass, but the end is not yet. For nation shall rise against nation, and kingdom against kingdom: and there shall be famines, and pestilences, and earthquakes, in divers places. All these are the beginning of sorrows.

This is what I saw when I finished my speech and looked out at the audience: my father, leaving. He stood up and edged his way out of his row. Then—walking so rapidly up the aisle that it was just short of a run—he left. My father walked out, while Dr. Wyatt stayed, clapping mildly and politely with everyone else.

You'd have thought I'd be relieved—there was now no possibility of having to introduce my father and Viv. But I wasn't relieved. I felt weirdly chilled.

CHAPTER 7

AFTER OUR CLASS had flung their caps into the air—except for me; I fitted mine carefully above Viv's brow instead and, laughing, she was the one to hurl it aloft—the ceremony was officially over. Viv and I descended from the platform into the swarm of our fellow graduates' families and friends. Viv was immediately engulfed by her mother's embrace, while Bill, her mother's shy boyfriend, simultaneously wielded his video camera and hid behind it.

Mrs. Fadiman was sniffling. "My *baby*. You were so mature, so beautiful! And that thing you said, about facing life with kindness and courage, you can't possibly know that already, sweetheart, yet it was so true. Heads all around us were bobbing away in agreement, did you see? Oh, Vivian Elizabeth! You made me so proud, I thought I would die."

I hung back. I knew that shortly Mrs. Fadiman would be all over me, too. And also that she, like Viv, would soon be craning her neck, looking for my parents. Wanting to congratulate, to crow, to share. Wanting all the normal things.

I had kept an eye out during Viv's speech and afterward, just in case my father came back. He had not. But Dr. Wyatt's eyes stayed fixed on me throughout. Viv spoke forcefully and well, but he did not even once glance her way; I could feel his gaze on me even when I myself was watching Viv. When the caps sailed through the air, I looked at him directly again and saw him nod at me; saw him smile approvingly. Then, as everyone else applauded and yelled and whistled, he, like my father, got up from his chair in the audience and strode away.

Leaving me . . . groping.

Okay. There was some history between my parents and Dr. Wyatt, some joint past. That I already knew. There was the letter's mention of Dr. Wyatt: He had somehow facilitated my father's test for Huntington's. And now my father had looked at Dr. Wyatt half an hour ago and become angry—angry enough to walk out on his son's graduation as soon as his son had finished speaking. Why?

I remembered the single time my mother had with sanity mentioned Quincy Wyatt's name to me, years ago, when I had studied his work at school. The little scene had come back to me with extraordinary vividness when I had read the letter. *We used to know him,* my mother had said, at dinner. *Before you were born, when we were graduate students.*

My father had interrupted. He had taken her out of the room to talk. His voice had been low, but I have sharp ears. *I don't want to hear his name, Ava, and I don't want Eli hearing*

*it, either. It's dangerous. Bad enough he lives so near; bad enough
Eli is studying him at school.*

My mother had been impatient. *Oh, Jonathan. You make too
much of it.*

*And you promised we would never speak of it, or him, once it
was over.*

My mother had sighed, but said, *Okay. Fine. It doesn't really
matter, I suppose.*

Whatever had happened long ago . . . my father was angry
about it. But my mother hadn't been. And Dr. Wyatt wasn't.

Did you know my mother?

Nice woman.

I felt my shoulders move uncomfortably as, finally, the obvious explanation occurred to me. Had my mother once had
an affair with Dr. Wyatt?

For a few seconds I couldn't draw breath. You think you're
sophisticated. Mature. But some things . . .

"Eli!" Mrs. Fadiman abandoned Viv and moved to embrace
me. It was a huge relief to be distracted. Also, there was no
way not to like Viv's mother, no way not to respond to the
outpouring of approval she always directed toward me.

Impulsively, I picked Mrs. Fadiman right up off her feet—
she was even shorter than Viv—and whirled her around in a
circle. She laughed the twin of Viv's giggle, and I laughed
back down at her and whirled her again.

On my side, the laughter was partly manic. I knew my ugly
explanation had to be right. Whether I liked it or not didn't
matter. It had to be dealt with, if I was going to work at
Wyatt Transgenics.

I could confront my father and ask. I could even quit the job at Wyatt Transgenics, if he really wanted me to. I didn't want to do that, though. I wanted the job. But how could I take it if doing so really would cause my father pain?

But maybe it wasn't true.

"Stop! Enough! You'll make me dizzy!" Mrs. Fadiman was still laughing. Carefully, I set her back on the ground. She reached up and patted my cheek, said, "Young man, you need to shave," and then, looking around, added, inevitably, "By the way, where are your parents? Viv said they'd be here today."

My mouth opened automatically to speak, but nothing came out at first. "Um," I managed finally. "My parents . . . my father was here, but . . ."

"He had to leave early, after Eli spoke," Viv inserted quietly.

She was standing two feet away. My eyes met hers—one moment of complete clarity and understanding—and then she looked away. She added doggedly: "There was—um, a family emergency. A cousin, isn't that right, Eli? A cousin who was in a car accident this morning, and Mrs. Samuels is with her at the hospital, and Mr. Samuels went to join her."

Too much, Viv, I thought.

"Oh, my!" exclaimed Mrs. Fadiman. "How terrible!"

I managed to nod. By force of will I tried to make Viv look at me again. If she would just look at me.

Mrs. Fadiman said something else. I wasn't sure what it was. I spoke randomly. "She's going to be okay, my cousin. It's just that she needed, um . . ."

"Emotional support," Viv said.

"Of course," said Mrs. Fadiman. "But what a shame, to miss any part of your graduation. Bill will have the video, of course, and we can make copies, but it's not the same."

Viv had a smile pasted on her face. I felt the cloud of lies above our heads and knew that she felt it, too.

I knew then that this could not go on. Not if I wanted to keep her. But if I told her—well. I'd lose her, eventually, anyway. Either way. The truth was approaching like a train bearing down on a track to which I'd been tied.

All at once. Out of nowhere.

I caught Viv's eye again. I tried to tell her, silently, that my games were over. That soon, when we were alone . . .

It seemed she understood me. Her brow smoothed out. She tried to smile.

I tried to think of what I might say.

My mother is insane. It's a genetic problem called Huntington's disease.

It is untreatable and incurable.

There's a fifty-fifty chance I'll develop it, too.

Now can we please not talk about this again, or at least not until you're ready to break up with me? Which, by the way, you should do before you get too attached.

Because listen, Viv. This—you and me—isn't forever. When you fall in love and mate for life, when you have children, it won't be with me. I won't let it be. I know better than to hurt you that way.

I looked at Viv as I thought these things. She had never been more beautiful to me. And I realized that I knew exactly how she would react if she did know . . . and that I couldn't allow it.

I know better than to hurt you that way.

"Hello, hello!" came a booming voice. "There you are, Eli!"

And then suddenly, in front of us, his arms full of flowers, was Dr. Quincy Wyatt. "Hail the graduates!" he said, and pushed the flowers into the arms of an astonished Viv. "First rate," he said, turning to Viv's mother. "Just a first-rate valedictory speech from your daughter. Happy to meet you. Happy to meet any friends of Eli's."

He beamed upon us all. "May I take everyone out to an early dinner? To celebrate?"

CHAPTER 8

BUT I ENDED UP having dinner alone with Dr. Wyatt, while
the Fadiman contingent—with visible regret once they realized that the stranger with the flowers was the famous Dr.
Quincy Wyatt, my new employer—kept to previously made
plans. He took me to a small French bistro north of Harvard
Square called Chez Henri. It was early, just after five o'clock,
and we were the only diners in the restaurant. That felt strange
to me, but it didn't seem to matter to Dr. Wyatt. He ushered
me expansively into the dining room, employed his cane to
point out to the maitre d' the table he wanted, and then spent
sixty concentrated, silent seconds with the wine list while I
watched.

I tried to assimilate the fact that I was there at all. Dr. Wyatt
couldn't be this interested in every new laboratory assistant
that Wyatt Transgenics hired. It was—it had to be—my
mother he was interested in. His old lover?

What if he asked me about her? And yet . . . earlier, at my

job interview, he'd seemed somehow to know about her current condition. There had been sympathy in his face.

Was he sorry for me? Was that what all of this was about? Just general pity because he knew about my mother's illness?

He'd mentioned *both* my parents, back at the interview. I wondered: Why hadn't he asked me where my father was today? Had he seen my father leave? Or maybe he'd assumed my father was with my mother at the nursing home?

Wherever my father was, I knew he would be wondering where I was, too. I knew he would be angry. Wanting an explanation. And spoiling for a fight about my new job and about Dr. Wyatt.

Before coming to dinner, I hadn't called my father or left him a message about where I was going or what I was doing. I wouldn't call now, either. Let him stew. He'd walked out on my high school graduation . . . and even though I hadn't been sure I really wanted him there, even though I was glad to sidestep his meeting Viv, it still wasn't right of him to have walked out.

No. Actually, I just didn't want to tell him I was with Dr. Wyatt when I should have been with him. I was vaguely ashamed. But it wasn't my fault.

The waiter arrived with water and a bread basket. "Something to drink?"

I was about to ask for a Coke, but Dr. Wyatt waved the wine list. "We'll have this 1995 Brunello di Montalcino." He turned to me. "It's a nice Italian red."

"Uh, sure," I said after a second. I didn't want to appear unsophisticated, and if the waiter didn't notice that I was under the legal drinking age—and because of my size, people did tend to think me older than I was—I wouldn't mention it. It was only wine. Still, I wasn't sure I wanted to drink ever again in my lifetime. I hadn't had any alcohol since the night I had fought with my father, polished off his dusty bottle of scotch, and then emailed Dr. Wyatt.

Luckily the waiter had already provided big glasses of water.

"An appetizer?" asked the waiter.

"Let's try the coconut shrimp," said Dr. Wyatt. "And a plate of the frogs' legs. Oh, and maybe the blue cheese, pear, and walnut salad. Two plates and serving spoons so we can both try everything."

The waiter departed. I hoped I'd be allowed to choose my own dinner. I said to Dr. Wyatt, "Uh, I might not have any frogs' legs."

"Of course you will. You should go through life seeking out new and different experiences, especially when you're young. It broadens the mind. What? What's that expression? What are you thinking?"

I shrugged. "It's just that, well, you hear that a lot. About the importance of a broad mind. We hear it all the time at school, for example."

"So?"

"So—well, Viv and I—you met Viv today—had this conversation recently. Isn't it possible that there are times when you'd want people not to have broad minds? When it would be an advantage to be, oh, narrow and provincial?"

Dr. Wyatt leaned forward. "Such as?"

"Well, suppose it's wartime. If orders really need to be followed, then it would not be helpful for soldiers to have knowledge, say, of the enemy's culture. That knowledge would just make you feel terrible about what you have to do. And in some cases, it might make you question your orders—might make you disobey."

"Yes," Dr. Wyatt said. "It's one reason why military training de-emphasizes individuality and emphasizes the importance of the team, the group, and of the order of command. Following orders has to be made instinctual and automatic."

"Right," I said. The wine arrived and Dr. Wyatt went through the tasting ceremony with the waiter, who then deftly poured a glass for each of us. The whole process took time, and I found myself thinking that I couldn't remember how long it had been since I'd had an intellectual conversation with an adult.

Once upon a time, I'd talked with my parents this way, of course, but no longer.

Now I felt the words and ideas gather pressure inside me. Finally, the waiter left. Dr. Wyatt steepled his hands on the table and leaned toward me.

"So," he said. "You interest me greatly, Eli. Soldiers—you were saying . . ."

"That soldiers are better off without too much broadening," I said. "Or, at least that's what we would think. But I've wondered—listen, do you like science fiction?"

Dr. Wyatt nodded. "Most people in the sciences do."

"Okay, then, you have to have noticed that you just keep seeing book after book, movie after movie, TV series after TV series, with robots or androids or genetically created hybrids of some kind or other. Right?"

"Yes. Of course."

"And they're always created with the idea that because they're not human, they'll be terrific, sort of, servants and will do whatever is asked of them. They'll follow orders exactly and they'll perform perfectly." I gulped some of my water.

"Perfect soldiers, yes." I thought Dr. Wyatt's smile was a little indulgent.

I said, "Yeah, soldiers, a lot of the time. We're—Viv and I are fascinated with that. But—the thing I want to say—in the end, it doesn't matter what job it is we've imagined that these created beings will perform. The fact is, it never works out."

"Never?" said Dr. Wyatt quizzically.

"Never," I repeated firmly. "We dream about the perfect, narrow-focused creature, we say it's what we want. But then something always goes wrong—or right—in these stories, and the robots always develop independence and individuality and don't want to obey anymore. Always. From *Frankenstein* on."

"Hmm," said Dr. Wyatt. "You mean that they're searching for free will?"

"Well, yes," I said. "What Viv says is that these creatures actually develop a soul. Every time we try to imagine that ideal robot or whatever, that soulless creature, we fail. At some deep level, Viv thinks, we humans believe every being must have a soul. Or, I guess you'd say, we humans believe that every human-like creature must have free will—or whatever you want to call that unique something that makes us human."

"But I don't personally think that," said Dr. Wyatt. "I concede that most humans *like* to believe in free will. Or call it a soul, if you must. But free will is an illusion. All human decision-making can ultimately be traced back to material causes. One set of neurons fires instead of another—and so we go left instead of right.

"Now, the decision-making process is certainly more complex in humans than in other animals, but I don't really think there's any sharp dividing line distinguishing human moral choices from the kind of daily choices that are made by any animal." He shrugged. "Free will? The soul? Something unique in humans that separates us from animals? It's a fairy tale we've invented to shield us from reality."

His eyes sharpened on me. "Obviously, from what you've said, your girlfriend has some vested interest in believing this sort of thing. Many people do, and so what? But what about you, Eli? You're a rational being. You have some grounding in science, and not just science fiction written by—excuse me—nineteenth-century hysterics like Mary Shelley. What do you think? Does free will—the soul—some basic human essence—exist?"

I hesitated. Was he insulting Viv? But no—he didn't know her. This was an intellectual discussion only—and a fascinating one. What did I think?

I looked him right in the eye. "I think that, as a species, we visit this topic in fiction over and over not because—or not only because—we're obsessed with the human soul. I think that just gives us a framework for discussion. The real reason is because, as a society, we're on the verge of making the creation of life, by humans, reality. We're trying to find ways to talk about it with people who aren't necessarily able to understand the science—because we all have to participate. As a species, I mean. We all have to decide what's best to do." I wanted to add, *what choices to make,* but then I remembered that Dr. Wyatt had just said he didn't really believe in moral choice. Just in neurons.

"Aha," said Dr. Wyatt. Then he smiled. "I see. Well, you and I needn't use the made-up worlds of fiction in order to talk about humans creating life."

"Robots are real," I said. "Cloning of animals is viable. Human cloning—it's going to happen."

"Yes. Exactly! We're living in the most exciting period of human history. Incredible control, incredible power over our own destiny, is almost within our grasp. There's a wonderful world ahead—new mysteries unlock to our eyes every day. God created man?" His chin jerked up. "So what? We are going to be able to do that, too. And eventually—it will all take time—we'll do a better job at it."

I stared at him. Of course the idea wasn't new—but hearing it . . . hearing it from Quincy Wyatt . . . hearing it aloud . . . *Do a better job than God?*

"There's just so much wrong," Dr. Wyatt added quietly. "Disease. Suffering." His eyes were intense, but I had the sense he was looking inward. His voice was low. Sad.

"There so much wrong, Eli. There's so much human pain and anguish in this world that I believe needn't happen at all."

CHAPTER 9

IT WAS 9:30 WHEN I returned home from dinner, usually a time at which my father could be found in the living room, his feet propped on the coffee table as, simultaneously, he watched television and read. Tonight, however, the apartment was silent and almost completely dark. Almost. There was a sliver of light beneath the door of my parents'—my father's—bedroom at the far end of the hall.

I stood at the other end, next to the living room, and for some minutes looked at the crack of light spilling onto the dreary brown carpet. Then I turned away and went into the kitchen, flipping the light switch on, dumping my backpack on a chair, and opening and closing the refrigerator. I knew I was just moving around for the sake of moving around. I was still pretty wired from having that incredible dinner and conversation with Dr. Wyatt.

I opened the refrigerator a second time. Then I shoved the refrigerator door shut with my elbow. I knew the noise would be audible throughout the apartment—as had the noise of my key in the lock when I got home, and of my footsteps moving about ever since.

I was being ignored. And even though we'd been living very carefully together, my father and I, these past years, more roommates than family at times—I suddenly realized that never before had I come home and not gotten some kind of greeting. Even on the few occasions in the last year when I'd stayed out very late at Viv's. I'd come home those nights—trying to be quiet—and my father would always hear me. He would stick his head out into the hall, and say, "Good, you're home. Now go to bed."

He'd stayed up waiting those nights, I now let myself understand. He'd stayed up, with the light under his bedroom door like tonight, and he'd done that even though I wouldn't ever tell him where I was. Even though all I would say to him was, "It's nothing to worry about, not drugs or wild parties or drinking or anything."

I sat down heavily on a kitchen chair. I closed my eyes briefly and saw my father as he had been this afternoon, at the graduation, with his fury boiling off him as he strode up the aisle and away.

Dr. Wyatt had said how much he looked forward to my starting work on Monday. He had driven me home just now. Had my father heard his Lexus idling outside when I got out of it? Had he heard my voice saying good-bye, see you Monday?

It was a warm, pleasant evening. My father's bedroom windows faced the street.

I ought to have called him. I always called when I was going to be at Viv's.

Okay. I could go knock on his door now. I could just say—

Then I saw the note on the kitchen table: a single sheet of lined paper, folded in half. *Eli.* The letters were formed in my father's precise handwriting.

I snatched it up.

It's clear to me now that somehow you've gotten to know Quincy Wyatt, and that your new job is with Wyatt Transgenics. I don't want to know the details of how that happened. I don't care. I simply ask you not to take the job. In fact, I ask you not to let this man be in your life in any way.

I can't tell you why, Eli. But I am begging you to do what I ask, and to do it immediately and without question.

Love, Dad

I read the note three times. Then I sat quietly in the kitchen beneath the fluorescent light for a few minutes, until I was ready to go down the hall and knock on his door.

"Come in," said my father.

He was sitting up in bed, wearing shorts and a T-shirt, with a book in his hands. He said, "Have a seat. Just toss that stuff from the chair on the floor. I keep thinking I'll do laundry soon."

I heard myself say, "I could throw in a load now. I bet the laundry room is empty."

"No, I'll do it tomorrow."

We were silent. I moved his small pile of clothing from the chair to the floor and sat down. Then I blurted, "But I have to ask questions."

"No," said my father steadily. "I can't answer them."

"But if I'm giving up a good job—a job I think I'd really like—"

"Are you giving it up?" interrupted my father.

I shrugged uneasily. "I don't know. If you would only tell me what you have against him, maybe I would."

"No."

"I need a job. This is as good a job as I could hope to find."

"We're not discussing whether you need a job right now. I still think you should go to college in September. There are ways even now. But suppose I were to agree to your working—just for a year. There are people at Harvard I could talk to. There was a group of professors that your mother used to hang out with, and if I asked them to nose around, I'm sure we could find you a research assistant job there. After all, you're only eighteen. You're not qualified to do much more than wash beakers and enter statistics into the computer. You can do that anywhere."

"I'm told the job I'm starting at Wyatt Transgenics usually goes to college graduates with BS degrees."

My father's lips tightened. "Wyatt *would* say that. And it may even be true, but that doesn't mean the work at—that place—would be any more interesting or stimulating than—"

"It wasn't Dr. Wyatt. It was this woman in Human Resources." I hadn't thought of the cobralike Judith Ryan in days; it was weird to find myself speaking of her as if I'd been flattered by her or something.

"We're off track," my father said.

"Yes," I said.

A car came to a stop on the street outside; its engine idled for a few moments and then someone got out and slammed the door, and the car sped away.

"You'll call tomorrow," my father said. "You'll tell them you've changed your mind. You can talk to Human Resources. There's no need to talk to Wyatt."

"Did he know Mom?" I said.

My father stared at me.

"Were they lovers?" I said bluntly. "Is that why you're jealous? Did Dr. Wyatt and Mom . . ." I couldn't find the right verb. I shut up. I couldn't look at my father. I fixed my eyes on the book he'd been reading and was surprised to see that it was one of mine, from English class. Poetry by William Blake. *Songs of Innocence and of Experience.*

I could hear my father breathing shallowly.

"I'm sorry," I said after a while. "That stuff isn't my business. It's private. I shouldn't have asked."

"No," said my father.

"I'm sorry," I said.

"I mean no," my father said clearly, "they were not lovers. Never."

I looked up then. His face was as grim as the day we took her to the nursing home for good.

"And don't go thinking it was some hopeless crush on her part, either. Or anything romantic, on either side."

I wasn't sure I believed him. "Okay. Then what is it that has you so angry—"

"No! I said I won't tell you, and I mean it. I am simply asking you to quit that job and do something else. Anything else. Will you?"

I thought of my dinner with Dr. Wyatt. I thought of his face as he toasted my high school graduation. I thought of how we had talked for hours, how *he* had talked, about creation and the possibilities of the world we lived in—the scientific possibilities, the real possibilities, the possibilities that would soon no longer be confined to the imagination. I thought of the world that he knew, that I did not, but could. Could. A world that, before, I had barely dared speculate about. Could pain and suffering really be eradicated? Were the possibilities for humanity as limitless as Dr. Wyatt believed?

I thought, too—I must confess—of the high salary I would be earning, and of how adult and in control having this good job made me feel, and of how happy Viv had been to learn of the job. How impressed she'd been to meet Dr. Wyatt today. I'd need something to keep her impressed next year, when she was with all those smart kids at Brandeis and I was a dropout. I wanted to keep Viv—for a while, anyway. Until it was too unfair to her . . .

I had been silent too long.

"This conversation is over," said my father wearily. "Go do what you want."

Later on, I would remember that moment as the turning

point. Odd, because I'd have thought other moments would feel more decisive. But that was the one that stood out in my memory: the moment in which what I said, what I decided, was the single vital factor. The moment in which I stood with words—important, life-changing words—on my lips just waiting to come out.

I'll quit the job. I'll do what you ask, without any more questions. And you owe me.

But I didn't say them. Instead, I said, "I'm sorry, Dad. I want to do this. If it had been about Mom—well, I would have quit. But since you say it isn't . . ."

I waited. I gave him a chance to tell me what it was about.

He didn't. After a moment, he simply picked up the William Blake, opened it, and began to read.

I left his room, closing the door behind me. I went to mine. I sat there in the dark, on the edge of my bed.

I was sorry to hurt my father. But I wanted to know Dr. Wyatt. There was at that time no force on earth that could have kept me from getting to know Dr. Wyatt and the world that he was promising to me.

And so, the next Monday, I went to my new job at Wyatt Transgenics.

CHAPTER 10

"IT'S ALL ABOUT MILK, KID," said my new boss, Larry Donohue, MS Molecular Biology, as he led me down one of the labyrinthine interior corridors of Wyatt Transgenics and past yet another bank of vending machines. Larry had seen fit to inform me within two breaths of hello that he was "working on a PhD at MIT," but now, half an hour into our tour of the building, I found myself deciding that maybe he wasn't as pompous as that had made me think.

I was liking Larry. He seemed sort of—sunny. He bounced as he walked, even though he was wearing a pair of Reebok cross-trainers so decrepit that I couldn't believe they had any bounce left to them. The crown of his head barely reached my shoulder at the top of each hop. I tried to guess his age: maybe twenty-eight? Was that young to be doing what he was doing?

"Yep, milk. M-I-L-K," Larry sang, as if he were in a commercial for the Dairy Association. "Milk from rabbits, mice, cows. Especially rabbits and mice." He skipped a little bit as we turned a corner, and suddenly I knew that this job was going to be fantastic. Even if I was washing beakers and entering data into a computer.

I looked up and down the carpeted corridor, its stretch broken only by lab and office doors on either side. I sniffed and got only the scent of ammonia cleaner. "Mice and cows," I repeated. "And rabbits. I see."

Larry grinned up at me. "Well, of course this facility is mostly just labs and offices. Some of the mice and rabbits are here—the ones we're working with to develop new proteins, not the animals in active production. And we do have a milking room for the rabbits here, in the basement. It's kind of neat; the doe hangs out comfortably in a little sling while this vacuum tube apparatus does the milking by basically imitating the sucking of puppies. But we wouldn't dream of keeping any cows here. The big livestock is kept on the farm and dairy, out west." He waved an arm to the north. "Near Amherst. Probably you'll get out there one day to see that part of things."

"That would be great," I said. "And what do we"—I was surprised to hear how easily that *we* slipped out—"do with the milk?"

"Well, here's the deal." Larry stopped walking. "It's all about human protein development. Hey, what do you already know about this, so I don't waste your time?" He was too nice a guy to add, *or mine.*

"Pretty much nothing," I admitted. "Um—you probably know this—I'm just a high school graduate." I felt compelled to add, "I got this job as a—as a sort of favor, but I promise, I'm going to do my best here."

"Yeah," said Larry. "I'd heard that, uh, you were young." He gave me a sideways look. "You know Dr. Wyatt, I understand?"

I didn't know what to say. I half-nodded and half-shrugged.

"Lucky you," said Larry mildly. I still couldn't think of anything to say. I didn't have to, though. Larry simply continued talking.

"Well, I'll give you some books and articles to read, but here's the short story. You know what 'transgenic' means? It's when an organism is altered by having a gene from another species transferred into it. Transgenic research involves studying organisms that have undergone this kind of manipulation. Clear so far?"

We had started walking again. I had a very unscientific urge to mention Spider-Man, who had been bitten by a radioactive spider. X-Men. Behind that silliness was the same idea, I now realized—the transfer of genetic material. Transgenics. Perhaps the very key to the end of suffering that Dr. Wyatt had talked about. "I get it," I said.

But it was as if Larry had read my mind. "Take the Swamp Thing. You know him? Half-plant, half-man?"

"Yeah," I said. Then I added gravely: "It was a terrible accident in the laboratory."

"It's *always* a terrible accident in the lab." Larry placed a hand over his heart. "Or sabotage." Then he grinned. "But hey, Eli, did you read the issue where we found out that wasn't *quite* what happened?"

"To tell you the truth, I just saw the movie. Years ago."

We had reached our own home lab, on the east side of

the building. Larry waved me through the doorway and followed, bouncing again. "Oh, and there was a TV series, too. On cable. Anyway, get this. Turns out Dr. Alec Holland actually *died* before he fell into that swamp. His corpse decomposed and got eaten by the swamp plants at the bottom. The plants absorbed the super-growth plant formula—remember, Dr. Holland was covered by it in the explosion?—and the plants became intelligent. Get it? The plants actually figured out how to mimic a human body in plant form. The plant creature thought it was Dr. Holland! So, Swampy isn't a man who's turned into a plant. Swampy's a plant that tried to become a man."

"Vive la différence," said a voice behind us.

"This is relevant, Mary Alice," said Larry. "Okay, introductions. Mary Alice Gregorian, Eli Samuels. Eli, Mary Alice actually runs this particular lab on a day-to-day basis; sets the schedules and so on, while I focus on directing our research path."

Mary Alice was a middle-aged woman with a long braid of hair. She had a pair of plastic goggles dangling around her neck. We shook hands. "I'll show you the rabbits," she said. "We'll put you on feeding, care, and milking rotation after you learn how to work with them."

"Rabbits," I said. Well, it wasn't cleaning beakers. "Huh."

"Try to contain your enthusiasm," said Larry. "You'll like them. They're cuddly, and, well, you get used to the pellets."

"They are *sooo* cuddly," said Mary Alice. "But it's important to remember they're research subjects, and very valuable. They're not pets."

"I was actually just explaining our research to Eli," Larry said to Mary Alice. "Swampy came up in passing."

"He always does." Mary Alice directed my attention to the far wall. Above a computer desk hung a Swamp Thing poster, meticulously matted and framed. On it, a giant leafy hand was emerging from murky water; above that were the words: *Too intelligent to be captured. Too powerful to be destroyed.*

"So much weirder than Batman," murmured Mary Alice.

Larry practically choked. "Mary Alice, you don't understand this and you never will. Batman's nothing to do with transgenics. He has no genetic enhancements. He's just plain psychotic."

Mary Alice rolled her eyes. "Sorry."

"You should be." Larry sat down. Then I saw a secret smile creep over both their faces and realized I had been watching a little routine between them, a skit that they both enjoyed and probably repeated regularly, whenever there was a new audience—like me.

"Anyway," Larry said to me. "As I was saying. Here at Wyatt, we're using transgenic technology to develop human proteins outside of humans—proteins that can then be harvested and used in humans. The potential medical and therapeutic benefits are mind-boggling. It's not a unique idea. Other companies, like Genzyme, are doing it, too—although they're really into working with goats. But we think we've got the inside track right now, especially with rabbits."

Mary Alice said, "We give the transgenic genes—genes that originate in humans—to the animals. The genes cause the animals to express certain human therapeutic proteins in their milk. Then we milk the animals, and purify the proteins out of the milk. The resulting proteins can then be used in a variety of medical applications."

"Like what?" I asked.

"Treatments for arthritis," said Larry. "Cancer. Several conditions that attack the immune system. And that's only for starters—once you begin thinking about the potential, well, your brain starts to reel. And even the animal rights people can't complain—I mean, we're talking *milk* here. Our animals lead good, useful lives. They're valuable to us, and we treat them well. We're lucky; so many areas of biogenetic research are fraught with controversy, but ours hasn't really had to take those kinds of PR attacks."

I nodded. I couldn't think of any reason why this sort of work shouldn't be done, either. It certainly wasn't full of the kind of potentially treacherous moral issues that I'd been discussing with Dr. Wyatt the other night, as we spoke about free will and human genetic destiny. "It's pretty impressive, what you do here," I said, and meant it.

In actual fact, Larry and Mary Alice hadn't told me anything that I didn't already know, from researching Dr. Wyatt and from reading the company's promotional literature on their website and in my employment packet. But it was different, hearing it from the people who worked there, hearing it while standing in the lab where I myself was going to work.

I belong here, I thought. I really do. Larry is even interested in the same superhero stuff that Viv and I talk about. I bet Viv would like to talk to him sometime about her soul theories.

I was full of eagerness and excitement.

"Come meet the rabbits," said Mary Alice. "And I'll explain to you about the specific proteins that we're hoping to get them to express."

"Let's go," I said.

CHAPTER 11

IT WAS A GOOD WEEK, a rare week. I found myself springing from bed each morning like a piece of toast from the toaster, and my legs seemed to have made an independent decision to run all the way to work. On Thursday, after two consecutive mornings of waiting outside our lab door for someone to arrive and unlock it, I was presented with an access card key of my own, and the next morning, well before nine a.m., I had fed all of the Flopsy, Cottontail, MarchHare, Foo-foo, and Bugs rabbits (there were several with the same names, distinguished by numerical suffixes), recorded the weight of their feces, and set aside sections for routine analysis. In the late afternoon, I had to be shooed out, and I had so much to tell Viv, I thought I would explode before I could see her.

I love this, I thought. I love being an adult.

I was so happy that it even crossed my mind to try to talk to my father, to let him know how good a decision this had been. But there was no sense tampering with the silent truce at home. No, it was enough that my father had wordlessly agreed to just let me do what I had decided to do. I wouldn't ask for more—wouldn't risk more conversation—and, maybe, neither would he.

If I also kept wondering what my father was concealing about Dr. Wyatt, what he had against him, I didn't let myself dwell on it. I was well practiced in not dwelling on things . . . and despite my father's denial, I continued to believe this had something to do with my mother.

I cleaned out rabbit cages with zeal, and created a new computer report that sorted the historical data over animal generations and was easier to read.

"All this youthful enthusiasm," Larry said to Mary Alice. "It will wear off. Please, tell me it will wear off."

The only thing keeping the job from complete perfection was the fact that I hadn't seen Dr. Wyatt. I routed my steps past his office three or four times that week, but his door was always closed, and I didn't hear from him.

I tried to reason away my disappointment. He was a busy man, and he'd already done so much for me. It was ridiculous of me, juvenile, to have expected anything more, no matter what he'd implied about seeing more of me, having more conversations, even—did I dare hope for it?—acting as a mentor.

Judith Ryan in Human Resources made that perfectly clear on Friday afternoon, when I went there to drop off signed employment forms and to watch a video for new employees about retirement savings and stock option plans. On my way out—even though I knew better—I stuck my head in her office, said a tentative hey, and waited for her to raise her cobra head. Which, eventually, she did.

I'd been planning to be offhand and casual, but under her stare it was not possible. "Remember me? Dr. Wyatt brought me down here to meet you? I'm working with Larry Donohue now. I just started this week . . ." I had an impulse to add that it turned out that Larry liked to make jokes about microbes, but managed to restrain myself.

"You have a question?" said Judith Ryan.

"I was just wondering if Dr. Wyatt had left a message for me down here. Welcome to the company or something, or—or maybe he wants to have lunch one day and couldn't find me . . ."

"I assure you that if Dr. Wyatt wants to see anyone who works here, he can find them." Without waiting for a response, she turned and reached for the lower drawer of a file cabinet.

I slunk away.

And then it was Saturday. Nursing home visit day. And yes, I know a good son would have gone daily, but I couldn't bear to, lately. I had hit some kind of emotional wall last winter, and couldn't make myself visit her any more often than once a week. My father could have insisted, and we both knew it. But he did not. He said it was my decision. In a secret, irrational part of my soul, I hated him a little for that. I hated him for it every time he went to see my mother, while I went to Viv to hide.

If Viv ever met my mother, she—even she, even sweet, generous, intelligent Viv—would stiffen in horror and revulsion.

"Hello, Mom," I said. I found her with an aide on the airy screened porch of the nursing home. She was sitting in the big padded expensive wheelchair that protected her somewhat as the muscles all over her body and face twitched erratically. "It's a beautiful day," I said with that falsely cheerful note in my voice. "The lilacs are blooming. There's a big set of bushes just outside. They smell incredible."

I pulled out the three-ring binder that I'd retrieved from her room. I opened it to the laminated page of photos of me. Me as an infant; me as a toddler; me at ten, twelve, fifteen. Beneath the photos we had printed my name in large letters. I held the page up before her. "Eli," I said. "It's Eli visiting you, Mom."

I had no idea if she recognized me, or the photos, or the word *Eli* anymore. I didn't even know if she'd recognize the page of photos of herself.

"She's just been unfortunate," the neurologist had told us. "The—" He had paused for a second, searching for a word other than *insanity*. "—final deterioration associated with Huntington's disease doesn't always happen this rapidly."

I remembered staring at him, wondering if it would actually have been better to have more years with my mother in which the so-called early stages of HD dominated our lives. I remembered something I'd read in the HD literature. *Intellect is not affected in the early stages, only access to the information.*

Better or worse, to have things happen so fast with her? Better for her, worse for us? The reverse? I didn't know.

Or maybe I did. Maybe I was glad she couldn't live with us now. Maybe I was glad it would be over—relatively—soon. Weeks, or months, at best.

I knew I was glad that her rages had slowed and softened, becoming sad rather than dangerous. Glad that, because of her total inability to keep her balance, she could no longer walk at all. Glad even for the stupors she fell into now, in which she was totally alien, totally unreachable.

Evil thoughts. I know. I know.

I know.

The mass of twisted muscles that was my mother twitched and jerked beneath the soft blue cotton wrap dress she'd been put in that day.

"Shall I leave you two alone for an hour or so?" asked the aide.

"Okay," I said, as I always said, even while I wanted to scream *no*. "I know where to find you if I need you. All right if I wheel her out into the garden?"

"Good idea," said the aide. Her name was Patty, I recalled as she walked away. It was too late to use the name to her, of course.

I could never easily remember the names of anyone who cared for my mother, even in the early days, back when we lived in a big house near Harvard Square, back when my mother was only experiencing clumsiness . . . then having weird, frightening mood swings . . . and walking so oddly, as if she were drunk. Then, one time, she pulled every glass out of the cabinets and threw them violently at my father and me.

I was thirteen.

After that, a nurse had moved in with us for a while, until a nursing home could be found. I could never even remember that live-in nurse's name. Felicia? Francesca? I had some kind of mental block about it.

Unless the memory problems were an early symptom of HD in me. Early onset or juvenile HD. It wasn't supposed to happen so early, it was highly unusual, but . . . it could. It was possible.

In my regular life, I tried not to think about it, but when I visited my mother, it was impossible to escape the disease's shadow, its questions. I even sometimes believed that I could tell that the nurses and aides and doctors were thinking about it as they looked at me. I could hear their voices, whispering.

Her son. Eli Samuels. Of course he has the usual chance of inheriting HD himself. What a terrible disease. Nothing to be done . . . you can take the test nowadays and find out if you have it or not, but if you do have it, then you just wait for the symptoms.

No treatment. No cure.

If I were in her shoes, I wouldn't have had children at all. She must have known she was at risk, even if the test wasn't yet available. How could she put her own child at risk, too? How could her husband?

I wonder if the boy will take the test to find out? You can take it anytime after you're eighteen. There are reasons not to. I mean, what kind of a life can you live, if you find out at eighteen or twenty that you're going to get HD at thirty-five, or forty, or fifty . . . sometime. How can you live with the certainty that you'll get it, that only the timing is unclear?

Imagining their voices, imagining what they were thinking—knowing that it was really what I was thinking myself, the beginning of what I was thinking, deep down, deep down in the places I didn't want to go—made me feel . . . well. It made me feel insane.

I thought about my father's HD-negative test letter. Someday I would ask him about it . . . someday. I found that I was not feeling so angry about it anymore. He, like me, like my mother, had been at risk. Now that I had absorbed the shock of that, it was easier to accept. Maybe their vulnerability and uncertainty about the future had been something he and my mother had shared, something that had made them feel closer to each other, love each other. Maybe it was why he had been able to remain with her and take care of her when she began to be symptomatic. Maybe, for my father, it had been, *There but for the grace of God, go I*. I could respect that. I could respect his privacy and his choices—even if I didn't yet know why he'd made those choices, or even why he'd used Dr. Wyatt as an intermediary when he took the test.

Maybe it was easier, too, to accept others' actions if you believed, as Dr. Wyatt did, that there was no free will.

My head cleared a little in the open air. I wheeled my mother down the path into the garden. Pushing her chair was good; I felt active, and I didn't have to look at her much as I talked. I told her the plot of a movie I'd seen on TV the other night. I told her about a new building, a skyscraper, that they were putting up in Boston. She used to be very interested in architecture.

I didn't say anything about my father to her, or about Viv, or about me. I didn't mention my new job, or Dr. Wyatt, or anything real in life. What was the point? What was the point of pretending that Ava Louise Lange Samuels was someone who meant anything in my day-to-day life?

Nowadays she was kept very much in a drugged state anyway.

I parked her wheelchair next to a bench and sat down beside her. I took out the three-ring binder again, planning to open it to the page of pictures of food. For a second, as I flipped through the binder, I saw the page of pictures of her when she was well, when she was beautiful. *Ava,* it said at the top of the page. *You,* it said at the bottom. In the middle was a picture of her on her wedding day—and one of her holding me on a bicycle. My first two-wheeler. She looked very serious. I could even remember her explaining the principles of propulsion to me.

I found the food page. *Sandwich. Pizza. Chicken. Cookie.*

"What do you think?" I pointed to the picture of a slice of chocolate cake. "Should I run over to the bakery and get some cake for us to have after lunch?"

I watched her face closely. I thought she nodded, but I might have imagined it. It hardly mattered, though. I was only pretending to be a caring son. I was not.

I wished she were dead. I wished she were no longer suffering. I didn't know anymore if I wished this for her sake, or my father's, or my own.

"Terrific, Mom," I said. "Cake it is."

CHAPTER 12

As USUAL, AFTER leaving my mother, I began to run the three miles home rather than take the bus. Passing one of the middle schools, though, I got lucky: A bunch of men in their twenties were playing basketball on the playground court. I joined them for a while, and I must have been even more agitated than usual after a visit, because for once I found myself playing nearly as aggressively as I could. One of the guys fell backward onto the asphalt when I jumped in front of him to snatch the ball.

For a second I thought he was really hurt—there was a bemused look on his face. But it was okay; he got up and laughed and asked me where I played college ball. "I was a guard at BC," he said with a proud little jerk of the chin. But then, just as I opened my mouth to say that was cool, he added quickly, deferentially, "But I wasn't a starter."

The other guys had gathered around. They were regarding me with interest.

"You're a center, right?" said this guy. "Where do you play?"

The back of my neck was prickling with warning. All I'd wanted was a pickup game. A little exercise. A little forgetfulness. I looked around at the group of men. They seemed assured, confident—young lawyers and medical students and computer guys and businessmen, I guessed. Well-educated, healthy, well-off; the world open before them.

I thought of the basketball coach at my high school; he'd bugged me pretty much continually, freshman and sophomore year. But I kept telling him no and finally he gave up.

"No," I said easily to these guys. "I'm not in college. I don't play for anybody. I just like a casual game now and then."

There was a pause. Then: "Oh," said the man who'd fallen, a little over-heartily. "Well, what a shame. I mean, you're a natural, and when you think of all those scholarships, it's just too bad . . ."

I shrugged. I dribbled the ball, backed up to pass. "Right. Let's go, okay?"

We got back into it. I was more careful now; making sure to pass the ball often, jumping less, not dominating the game. At the end, they asked me to come back next Saturday and I smiled, shook hands, said maybe.

But I knew I wouldn't. I think they knew, too. I think they were glad to see me go.

I started walking home again.

Much as I liked playing team sports, I usually just didn't. Somehow things always got strange.

I remembered way, way back, when I was six or something, playing soccer. My realization that the other kids made mistakes—and that I didn't. And the way people began whispering, looking at me. The admiration and anxiety of the other kids. The interest from the coaches and the other adults. I ought to have liked it, maybe, but I didn't. I couldn't. Little as I was, it made me afraid. Somewhere in me, I thought it was a bad idea to draw too much attention. To have people watch me too closely. And so one day I told my parents that I didn't want to play sports anymore.

I remember my dad looking at me. "Okay," he said. I had been prepared for him to ask questions, or to protest, but he hadn't. "If that's what you want," he said.

Of course, after my mother became symptomatic, there wasn't time for organized sports. At school, I hung out with nerdy unathletic types like Viv. And after a while, despite my size, nobody thought about me as a potential jock anymore. And except when something like this pickup game happened, I rarely thought about it myself.

It wasn't like I didn't get any exercise. I ran a few times a week, and in the summer, I liked to kayak. I played the occasional, slightly careful game of tennis on the courts at the Y in the summer, when they had open sign-up for games. It was enough. It was okay.

Inevitably, my thoughts drifted back to my visit with my mother—and the testing thoughts that seeing her always stirred up. My eighteenth birthday had been back in March. Of course, that was before I'd found the HD-negative letter addressed to my father, before I knew that he, too, had been at risk.

Things had been tense between us, anyway, about other things. I'd made sure I was busy with Viv on my birthday, but afterward I'd come home and my father had laid out all the genetic testing information on the kitchen table.

Just as I'd known he would.

The first step: the phone number to call to schedule the psychological counseling that they wanted you to have before you were tested, to make sure you could handle the results, either way.

I'd felt my father come up behind me. I hadn't turned around. My voice was steady.

—*Dad, listen. I don't think I want to know. I'm not ready. At least not now, and maybe not ever.*

—*But I'm sure . . . I tell you, Eli, I'm sure that you're negative. Just do this. Put your mind at rest.*

—*You mean put* your *mind at rest.*

—*No! This is what's best for you. Get it over with. It'll be a huge relief when you know, when you see the results, that you can just get on with your life.*

—*I'm not ready.*

—*Please, Eli . . . trust me on this. I just know you're negative.*

—*But you can't be sure, Dad. It's fifty-fifty. That's a scientific fact.*

Unbelievably, after that, the conversation had degenerated into a childish bout of "I do know!" "You can't!" "I do! I sense it!" until finally we'd both stomped away, angry and frustrated. It had become yet another area of silence between us, but the phone number was tacked up on the bulletin board in the kitchen. I never looked at it, but I knew it was there.

Making that appointment was more than I could bear to do. More than I could risk. How could my father not even try to understand that? I couldn't understand his attitude, especially now that I knew he'd gone through the same thing himself.

Although . . . maybe that was why.

Thinking about it now, feeling my muscles tighten even more, I realized that despite the pickup game, I was still full of adrenaline. I needed Viv, and would see her tonight—we were going out for dinner—but today she was at her summer job, doing gardening for a local landscaper. I hoped she wasn't going to be working every Saturday this summer. Even if we made plans every Saturday night, that would be a little tough.

I needed Viv. I needed someone today. Someone. Right now. Someone . . .

I had reached Central Square. I was only a few blocks from home, and the remainder of the afternoon stretched before me. I wondered if my father was home, or if he had scheduled clients this afternoon at his office. If he were home, I could at least try to talk to him. I could, very delicately, just begin talking about my week at Wyatt Transgenics and see what developed.

I knew this was a bad idea. But I also knew that at some point, I'd need—I'd be unable to stop myself from trying to find out what my father had against Dr. Wyatt.

Why not do it today? Didn't it concern me, too? In fact, this morning at the nursing home, I had actually wondered what would happen if I showed my mother a picture of Dr. Wyatt. What if, next week—

No.

I took a deep breath. Okay, Viv wasn't around. My father was out of the question. More exercise was probably my best choice. I could go running for real, ten miles or more, as fast as I could. I could take a kayak out on the river. I could go to the YMCA and do a weight circuit.

Instead I sat down abruptly on a bench at a Central Square bus stop, pulled out my cell phone, and called information. And I should have been surprised, but somehow I wasn't, when I discovered that Dr. Quincy Wyatt had a listed Cambridge phone number.

The phone company was already connecting me. If I was going to hang up, now was the time—now, before it rang.

I didn't hang up. I felt my sweaty fingers clutching the phone as it rang once. Twice.

He answered.

"It's Eli Samuels, Dr. Wyatt," I blurted. "I'm wondering if you're available—that is, if you'd like to meet me this afternoon to talk? Maybe in Harvard Square? We could have coffee or something."

A pause. I could visualize Judith Ryan's sneer, and was filled with shame at my presumption. I was asking Dr. Wyatt to hang out with me as if he were a kid like me.

But then he replied, warmly, "Hello, Eli. What a coincidence. I was just thinking about you. In fact, would you like to come over for dinner tonight? I have a young friend visiting whom I think you should meet."

I almost dropped my phone. I was astonished—and incredibly pleased. And sorry. "Oh, no, I can't. I have a date with my girlfriend tonight. Viv, you know. But maybe another time—"

Dr. Wyatt interrupted. "All right, then why don't you come on over to my house now? It's a few streets north of Harvard Square. Let me give you directions."

CHAPTER 13

DR. WYATT'S DIRECTIONS took me to a large, meticulously re-stored yellow-and-green wooden Victorian house on Avon Hill—one of the most exclusive neighborhoods in Cambridge. Even in the days when my mother was earning a full salary as an economics professor at the Harvard Business School, we couldn't have afforded to live in a place like this.

Well, few could. The house was the kind of gracious, enor-mous old building that, all over the city, had been gutted and renovated into four or five separate condominiums. Buying an apartment in such a house would cost six or seven hundred thousand dollars. A whole house—I couldn't imagine. Mil-lions?

It was the kind of thing Viv might know. I would describe the house to her tonight.

I shouldn't have been so shocked. Dr. Wyatt was world-famous; he ran a large, profitable corporation. And for all I knew, he might have a private fortune besides; there was something so sophisticated about him, he probably had a wealthy background. It was just—I groped—the contrast to Dr. Wyatt's small cramped office at work. I'd assumed that he wouldn't care about his surroundings. That he'd live in some apartment more or less like ours, regardless of what he could afford.

The house even had grounds, sort of: a large, lush green lawn and flower beds, surrounded by a decorative iron fence. Land surrounding a residence was scarce in Cambridge; most houses were lucky to have handkerchief-size yards. This, by contrast, was the kind of place that Viv's employers at the garden center got seasonal contracts to keep beautiful.

My initial shame at having telephoned Dr. Wyatt today came back even more strongly. He wasn't some teenager to hang out with to stave off boredom! I stood on the sidewalk before the house and swallowed hard. It occurred to me that I didn't even know if Dr. Wyatt was married. I'd assumed he was not—something about him had made me assume that—but maybe he lived here with a wife and children, even grandchildren.

I hadn't even thought to shower and change before coming. Just because Dr. Wyatt had said "now" didn't mean I couldn't have said I'd come in an hour. I was only wearing a plain T-shirt and shorts and sneakers—and, worse, anyone would be able to smell the dried sweat from my just having played basketball. I was tempted to pull out my cell phone again, call Dr. Wyatt, and make some excuse.

Just then, the front door of his house opened and a vision— a fairy princess in a white tennis dress—stepped firmly out onto the wraparound porch.

Long slender legs and arms extended smoothly from her minuscule dress. Silky brown hair cascaded gently to her waist. She reached up with one tanned bare arm and hand, pulled off a pair of sunglasses, and, cocking her head to the left, called to me. "Hey! We want to know if you're going to stand out there all day, or if you'll come in."

I got the eeriest sense of familiarity from her—as if I had seen her before in some dream. Then Dr. Wyatt appeared behind her, waving me toward the porch.

I had no memory of unlatching the iron gate and moving up the walk. Suddenly I was simply on the porch with them, being introduced, hoping that the vision didn't notice that I had to surreptitiously wipe my palm on my shorts before I could shake hands with her.

"Kayla Matheson," Dr. Wyatt was saying. "The young friend I mentioned on the phone. Her parents—old friends—have entrusted her to me for the summer while she does an internship at a Boston publisher."

I'd always thought those photos of models in magazines were airbrushed, but Kayla was living proof that they weren't necessarily a lie. I thought dizzily of a fawn . . . of an Arabian pony . . . some beautiful animal of fragile appearance, yet strong, leggy, vibrantly alive. Up close, I could see that she had the most amazing eyes: wide set, almost amber in color.

I had to say something to her or she'd think I was an idiot. "Publishing?" I asked. Why hadn't I showered before coming, why?

"I might want to be an editor," she said. "It's a possibility. Right now, though, I'm just an English major. I'll do the internship this summer and see what I think. Also, I'm going to be helping Q with his new book manuscript."

She called Dr. Wyatt Q? Weirdly, hearing that brought me back to myself a little. I turned to him. "You're working on a new book, Dr. Wyatt?"

"Yes. Not my usual university press sort of book. This is more popular science. I'm hoping to interest a wider audience, an intelligent educated readership—which is why Kayla will make the perfect assistant. She can tell me when I get too obscure or detailed. I wouldn't mind talking to you about it sometime, too, Eli. I think you'd be interested. The working title is *Genetics and Self-Control.* There are some relationships to the things we were discussing at dinner the other night."

I nodded. "Sure. I'd be flattered."

He smiled. "Good. That's a bonus. I have to admit that when you called a little while ago, my first thought was simply that you'd make good company for Kayla this summer. She only arrived a couple of days ago, and is already a little restless, I can tell."

"I've been wishing for someone to play tennis with," Kayla said. "Do you play?"

I had to look at her again, and the moment I did, I was lost. "Uh, yeah," I managed.

"Do you run?" she demanded next.

"Yeah."

"Excellent!" Kayla twirled toward Dr. Wyatt. "Q, you were right."

I glanced at Dr. Wyatt and found him looking straight back at me, an expression of contentment and approval on his face.

"Well, shall we go inside?" he said. "I believe I promised Eli some iced coffee."

Just then, Kayla tossed her head and some delicious scent wafted toward me from her hair. Ice, I thought. Yes. Please.

The house's interior was everything its exterior had promised. Kayla showed me around while Dr. Wyatt talked to someone named Raquel about the coffee. As a way to combat the effect Kayla was having on me, I tried to focus on the details of the house. Large rooms, opening gracefully off a big central foyer with a staircase. Shining wood floors, even in the kitchen. Walls painted strong colors: navy blue, bloodred. Tall bookcases built in everywhere, and crammed with books. Big airy open windows that ran almost floor to ceiling. Heavy wide sofas and chairs that were slipcovered in cotton, and solid-looking tables of mahogany and oak. Oriental rugs.

Everything gleamed.

Kayla paused halfway up the wide staircase in the foyer. From where I stood at the bottom of the stairs, I could see a cushioned window seat beneath an oval abstract stained glass window on the landing above. "Don't you want to see Q's office and the bedrooms?" she asked.

I was curious to see if Dr. Wyatt's home office would be as messy as his one at work, or if it would be pristine, like this house. The two images, so different, still jarred me. But it was more important that I not see Kayla near any bed. "Not right now," I said. "I need to duck into the bathroom here." I turned my back to her. I felt huge relief the second I closed the door and was alone.

When I didn't have to look at Kayla, her effect lessened. I

could remember that fifteen minutes ago, she hadn't been in the world at all, as far as I was concerned. I reminded myself that I had a girlfriend, and that I preferred to run alone. And that I'd wanted to talk to Dr. Wyatt, to tell him about my week. That I'd wanted him to be my friend. How could I talk to Dr. Wyatt in front of her? It would be better, far better, if Kayla weren't here.

As I assembled this defensive edifice, I whipped off my T-shirt, grabbed the soap, and washed up in the sink as well and as quickly as I could. Only when I was done did I realize that the soap was scented and that I now smelled like a floral arrangement.

I stared into the mirror. Viv thought I was good-looking. Hot. Was I really?

There was a soft rap at the bathroom door. "Eli?" Kayla's voice. "We're in the sunporch. Just through the kitchen?"

"Okay," I called. "Be right there." I realized that I still didn't know who else might be in this house. It was still a possibility that Dr. Wyatt had a wife and children.

But I didn't think so.

I looked again at my face in the mirror. I took a deep breath.

Then I went out to have iced coffee with Dr. Wyatt and Kayla Matheson.

CHAPTER 14

IT WASN'T THAT I forgot about my date with Viv that night. How could I forget? I had done all kinds of planning. I had gotten a reservation at The Top of the Hub, one of the most elegant restaurants in Boston. I had bought a nice linen jacket that actually fit, and had carefully tucked two hundred dollars in cash into my wallet. And Viv had told me four times about her new short black silk tank dress. "I've never worn anything like this before," she'd warned. "You'll die!"

There was no way I could have forgotten. I just . . . stood her up. Viv waited alone at the restaurant, all dressed up and perfumed, for two hours, from seven o'clock to nine o'clock that evening, and I never came.

I don't have an excuse, or an explanation that makes sense. I know my behavior was—unbelievable. Cruel. Or Viv's word: unforgivable. But it was just . . . it was that . . .

It was that, as afternoon faded into evening and I sat talking with Dr. Wyatt and Kayla Matheson on the sunporch, I was somehow unable to leave. I couldn't get enough of watching—surreptitiously—how the light from the sunset created a reddish shimmer around Kayla's hair. And the conversation flowed so easily between the three of us—Dr. Wyatt dominating, of course.

Was consciousness, self-awareness, something that really existed, or was it only the by-product of the operation of a certain type of computer, the human mind? And what about emotions? How did they come to exist?

And: "Eli, sit down. You can't leave yet," Dr. Wyatt said commandingly, the couple of times I made have-to-leave-now noises.

I didn't want to be rude to him. Or to Kayla.

And I thought that there was plenty of time. I lost track somehow. At first, it was still afternoon, and I wasn't supposed to meet Viv at the restaurant until seven. And she'd said, too, that she would probably be at least fifteen minutes late, that it would take her a while to get ready after a day spent mucking around with people's gardens and lawns.

If only I had arranged to pick her up at her home. At least she wouldn't have had to wait so publicly. But she had thought that I needed to be at the restaurant exactly on time to ensure we wouldn't lose our reservation.

So. What happened is that suddenly it was seven-thirty, and Dr. Wyatt was ushering Kayla and me through the house, saying the cook had prepared a lasagna and we'd be eating in the dining room. It was a special occasion, after all, with both of us young people there.

He just assumed I was staying for dinner. Even though I

had mentioned to him earlier that I was busy, he had forgotten. But that didn't matter. It was my fault. My fault, because I didn't do anything. I didn't say a word to Dr. Wyatt. I sat down at the dining room table and listened, and ate, and talked.

What was I thinking? Oh, any number of asinine things. That it would be rude to Dr. Wyatt and Kayla to turn on my cell phone—even though somewhere in me I knew Viv would be calling frantically. That I couldn't reach Viv if I tried, because she didn't carry a cell phone. Mostly, though, I was thinking that I'd just make it right with her later. I'd abase myself. Apologize. Make some excuse. This was Viv, after all. She'd understand about my not wanting to be rude to Dr. Wyatt. Viv always understood. She had not, after all, even said a single word about her disappointment when she hadn't met my parents at graduation. We'd gone on, since then, with things between us just the same as they had always been.

She'd figured out, I thought, that it was best not to rock the boat. Not to push Serious Discussions on me about abstract things like honesty and openness and trust that I didn't want to talk about.

And maybe, also, for a little while that evening, as I listened to Dr. Wyatt, as I stole glances at Kayla—maybe I did forget about Viv. Maybe I just really forgot.

This was Dr. Quincy Wyatt, after all. I was in his *home*. I was his *guest*.

And Kayla.

And then there was the conversation. Okay, it was more lecture than conversation. But that didn't matter; it was a lecture by Dr. Wyatt on the topics he planned to address in his new book, and I was privileged to hear it.

"Decades ago, Linus Pauling contended that scientists are obliged, in good conscience, to take an active part in forming public opinion in matters to do with science. I've come to see his wisdom on this point. We can't sit back and leave important science policy in the hands of politicians and pundits or"—there was the slightest glance at me—"alarmist writers of science fiction. Face it, most people are unbelievable idiots. They hear one poorly researched, supposedly balanced story on National Public Radio—on stem-cell research, for example—and they're arrogant enough to think they're now capable of making decisions that will influence the rest of humanity. Hogwash! They have no training in these areas. Their opinions simply should not matter."

Kayla prompted, "So, in your book . . ."

"In my book, I hope, I will convince the reading public that they ought to consult and trust scientists' opinions in many difficult scientific matters. And I hope, also, that I will convince my fellow scientists to eschew so-called 'political correctness' and speak openly those truths that they—that we—know are truths. To speak their consciences."

He went on, articulate, eloquent, and if I didn't quite understand what he was driving at when he spoke about politics and public policy—though Kayla seemed to—I didn't care. And one thing he said that night struck me so forcefully that I knew I would always remember it.

"Of course, it's impossible to work in biotechnology without being haunted by those famous words of Maurice Wilkins.

'DNA, you know, is Midas's gold. Everybody who touches it goes mad.'" He stopped talking for a moment, then repeated it, gravely, thoughtfully. "Midas's gold. Dangerous stuff, in short. And even an advocate such as I cannot deny that it behooves us to be careful, indeed."

When I left, and got into the cab that Dr. Wyatt had called for me, it was after ten o'clock. But I knew there was no way I could have left earlier. I couldn't have. I had been meant to be at Dr. Wyatt's house tonight. It was fate. I could go out with Viv anytime, after all.

But I would go see her now. I would apologize, and she would forgive me, and we would reschedule our dinner, and it would be no big deal.

I gave the cab driver Viv's address, and pulled out my cell phone to call her. But she wasn't at home. Only Viv's mother was there, at first relieved to hear from me . . . and suddenly screaming, exploding with how worried she and Viv had been—where had I been anyway?—and then, finally, answering my question and telling me where I would find Viv now.

At my apartment. With my father.

Mrs. Fadiman was going to call them right now and tell them to expect me.

CHAPTER 15

"I THOUGHT SOMETHING terrible must have happened to you!" Viv was wearing the little black silk dress that she had told me about, and she'd been right: It looked cute and sexy on her, even now, even though it was creased and sweaty. Nevertheless, Viv was a wreck. Her hair was crushed on one side; her mascara had smeared around her eyes. And suddenly—because of Kayla's perfection?—I could see all the little flaws. The askew mouth. The short waist. The uncared-for nails.

Guilt—and, shamefully, impatience—geysered up inside me.

"I'm sorry," I said for the umpteenth time. Of course she was entitled to hours of apologies, but I hadn't been permitted to say anything but "sorry, sorry, sorry" since I'd come in. For some reason this wasn't going as easily as I had thought it would.

Viv stood in the exact middle of our living room. She was clutching her arms in front of herself, cupping her elbows, glaring at me. Her mouth was trembling. "I'm sorry," I repeated to my father, who was leaning against the wall near the kitchen. The silence that followed let me think that I finally would be allowed to speak. "I didn't mean anyone to worry," I said. "It was—it was . . ." I discovered that I didn't, after all, have much to say. The excuses I'd been sure would occur to me when I needed them did not materialize. I found myself shrugging. "Something came up," I said, and I could hear the edge in my voice. So, I knew, could they.

Viv sank down onto the sofa. She had hugged me when I'd come in, but then she'd immediately backed off. "Why didn't you call?" she demanded now. "I was all alone at the restaurant, and I . . ." She bit her lip.

I desperately hoped she wouldn't cry. Not in front of my father. Then—the smeared makeup—I realized she probably already had.

This was unfair and wrong, I thought. The two of them in the room together—it was like worlds colliding, worlds I'd put so much energy into keeping separate. I had nothing to say to them. More, I didn't really even feel apologetic. Why should I answer to them? I'd been thoughtless, yes. But wasn't I allowed that now and then? Wasn't I allowed mistakes? By people who said they loved me?

Viv said, "I waited and waited, and finally I called your father and introduced myself." I heard the emphasis on the last two words clearly. She added, "He didn't know where you were, either."

There was a pause in which I could have said "I'm sorry," again, but I didn't. I looked at Viv and she looked at me.

"Let me guess," said my father. His voice could have competed with a desert for dryness. "You were at Wyatt's?" He was looking directly at me, and must have seen the acknowledgment on my face.

Viv gasped at my father. "If you knew that—guessed—why didn't you tell me? We could have called Dr. Wyatt—could have checked!"

My father said, very precisely, "I dislike Dr. Wyatt."

Viv's mouth fell a little open. "Oh," she said.

My father was still staring straight at me. "You acted like a cad tonight," he said. "I'm ashamed of you." Before I could reply—not that I had any idea what I would say—he levered himself away from the wall. "I'm going out," he announced. "Over to the Sheraton to have a scotch at their bar."

I turned and watched as he moved unhurriedly to the small table near the door and pocketed his keys. I watched his back as he opened the door and left. I kept watching the closed door as the silence came down around me and Viv and enclosed us. Finally, without looking at her where she sat behind me on the sofa, I said, "Viv? Want to take a walk? I can't stand being in this apartment right now."

She didn't reply, and in the end I had to turn to her. "Can we walk?" I asked again. I was trying now to temper the anger out of my voice. I still didn't fully understand where it had come from or why I felt it. With another part of me, I knew this was Viv—Viv, who I loved. That I wasn't really angry at her.

A whole minute passed before Viv shook her head. She leaned her elbows on her knees and her hands cupped her face. I could hear that she was wheezing.

I tried, then—a little.

I said, "We could go out tomorrow night instead. How would that be? I'd pick you up this time so you wouldn't have to wait anywhere."

Viv shook her head again. She leaned down further to conceal her face. Her shoulders shook, her breath heaved harshly—she was clearly trying not to sob aloud. "I'm sorry," she choked out. "But I am never going back to that restaurant." She curled further in on herself.

I knew I should sit beside her on the sofa and pull her into my arms. Stroke her hair. Say, "There, there." Murmur apologies and *never agains* and tell her I loved her over and over and over.

Instead I went looking for a box of tissues, didn't find one, and came back defiantly with a new roll of toilet paper.

Viv was still crying. I put the roll down on the coffee table in front of her. I watched her, this girl that I really did care for, who had truly been the only good thing in my life for the past year, and I felt incredibly distant from her.

My father was right, of course. I knew it. I had acted like that old-fashioned thing, a cad. Thoughtless, rude, cowardly, stupid. No argument. I should have fallen to my knees before Viv and begged forgiveness for hours. I should have been cuddling her right now.

But I was so tired. And it all suddenly seemed melodramatic and unnecessary—the apologies, the explanations. Games, theater, hoop-jumping. I had apologized already, several times. Was it really necessary that I abase myself? I would never make her do that, if the situation were reversed. Couldn't this just be over? Couldn't she be generous enough to forgive me easily? Did she have to cry? Did she have to be so . . . so manipulative?

I liked having a girlfriend. But for a second I wondered: What would it be like to have one who wasn't so emotional? Someone with whom I could just, oh, play tennis?

I hunkered down on the opposite side of the coffee table from Viv. Finally she stopped crying. She looked up. I handed her the toilet paper roll and she looked at it, then at me, and then tore some paper off and blew her nose. "Sorry," she said. "I'm a mess."

"I'm the one who should be apologizing," I said, not because I felt it, but because it was what I was supposed to say.

Viv shrugged. She got up and disappeared into the bathroom. When she came out, her face was scrubbed and she didn't sit back down. She said baldly, "I wasn't crying about tonight. I know you think I was, but I wasn't. Even though it was awful. Almost unforgivable, except for— I was crying— oh, Eli. Your mother. Oh, Eli. I am so sorry."

My mouth dropped open. I had been totally blindsided. I stared at her, not believing I'd heard what I'd heard. She knew. She knew—

All at once, rage was there. Swelling in me. Ready to boil over. Ready to—

"I asked your father about her tonight, while we were waiting," Viv said starkly. Compassionately. "He told me everything. Oh, Eli—"

Ready to explode.

I cut her off. "Well, congratulations. Now you know. And you also know that I didn't want you to know. I didn't choose to tell you myself. Not yet, anyway."

"But, Eli—"

"You didn't care about that, though, did you? You took the first opportunity you had to go poking around. You went behind my back. How does it feel? Huh? How does it feel to know? Are you happy now?"

"It's not like that! I was worried, I—"

"You were curious. It had nothing to do with being worried."

"But it did!" Viv was white. "How can you accuse me like this? It was all mixed up together. I had to call your father because I was worried about you, and I came over here to wait with him—he asked me to, if you care to know—and—"

"And you seized the opportunity to ask where my mother was. You couldn't wait to find out."

"But it wasn't to be nosy! It was . . ." She faltered.

I waited. I could feel the sneer on my face.

"It's because I care about you! I love you! I needed to know—I knew there was something going on. Something awful. I had to find out. You needed to trust me and you didn't. But you *can* trust me. I'll show you—"

I could hardly believe that the voice that lashed out whiplike into the air was my own. "You think I'll trust you now?"

Viv's hands groped behind her and pressed up against the wall. Her back collapsed against it. It was almost the exact same spot where my father had stood, half an hour ago.

"Eli. Please. I only thought—"

I had never felt so cold. "Vivian. You didn't think. Or you thought only about what you wanted. You ignored what I wanted. You trampled on my privacy. So listen to me now, because this is the only time I am going to say it.

"I do not want tourists in that part of my life."

Ten full seconds of silence ticked by.

Then Viv whispered, "I'm not a tourist. I love you. This is so terrible . . . I've read about Huntington's. I know a little bit. I'll learn more. I want to share this with you. Let me. Please. Please."

She was reacting exactly the way I had known she would. I noted the fact like a scientist.

"I don't want to share," I said. "My father got to share. I wanted to keep you out of it. That was what *I* wanted."

We stared at each other.

"But love is about sharing," Viv said, after a moment.

"No," I said. I could hear the conviction—and the raw anger—in my voice. "Love is about protection."

"No," Viv said frantically. "That's all wrong! You're wrong, wrong!"

"You're the one who's wrong," I said.

I think we both knew at that second, as our words hung in the air between us, that there was nothing more to be said. After all there had been between us—nothing.

I don't really remember the minutes that followed. But, finally, it was over. Viv's cab came for her, tooting from the street below. Upstairs, there was no slamming of doors or anything like that. Viv and I even hugged each other for a few seconds, though I felt as if I were made of stone. I kissed her on the brow. Then I sat in the living room and listened. I heard the cab's engine noise fade as it drove away.

I felt a strange kind of peace, because I knew I had done the right thing, even if in the entirely wrong way. Viv would know that, too, shortly. Shortly, she'd thank her lucky stars to have been extricated from me so easily. She'd read up on Huntington's—I knew Viv, and that I could count on—and she'd be horrified and pitying, and beneath that, even if it took her years to realize it, relieved.

Some things were not meant to be shared. Could not be shared. Even if she never admitted it, she'd know. She'd read and she'd know.

This was for the best.

I stood in the shower for a long time. Then I went to bed. Of course, I didn't sleep well. I never did, alone.

CHAPTER 16

As SOON AS THE sun came up the next morning, I went running beside the river. I threw my whole body into an outright run. But I was aware, as my legs pumped and my feet pounded and my heartbeat and breath steadied into an easy, regular, fast rate, that the endless length of a summery Sunday—a perfect blue-skied day—stretched out horribly before me. Empty.

I sprinted faster, rounding the curve past the old Harvard boathouse and heading across the Charles River to the Allston side.

I could call Kayla Matheson later. I could ask her to play tennis this afternoon. I was fairly sure that she—and Dr. Wyatt—expected me to call today. If it hadn't been said straight out yesterday, if an explicit date hadn't been made with a time and day attached, it had been implicit. It wouldn't be great exercise—which was a pity, because right now I felt like I couldn't get enough—but that wasn't the point. And, I told myself, there would be no need to feel guilty about seeing Kayla now that things were over between me and Viv.

It was a funny thing. Kayla was beautiful. I could tick off item by item those things about her that were so amazingly inviting: her lithe figure, sexy hair, creamy skin. And she was no airhead, either. But right this second the pieces wouldn't come together in my mind. I couldn't picture her, just her parts. Couldn't feel her attraction; only knew it had been there. Whereas Viv—being without her last night . . . right now I couldn't believe I had been so damned stupid.

No. I didn't need to think about Viv, and I would not. Would. Not.

She knew. She knew about my mother, and that was that.

Twelve miles later, I wasn't tired, but the path along the river was now crowded with fitness-minded Bostonians and Cantabridgians, and I realized that even if I didn't want breakfast, I ought at least to drink some water. I headed back to the apartment. Only as I came in did I realize what—who—I'd really come back for.

My father was reading the newspaper and drinking coffee in the kitchen. We said nothing to each other as I stood by the sink and downed three glasses of water, one after another. Then I turned and looked at him.

"Okay," I said. "I can feel you thinking it, so just say it right out loud."

"You dumped her last night, didn't you? That nice girl."

It wasn't his business. Besides, he already knew. But he kept looking at me, and so finally I said, "Yeah, I—we—broke up."

He slammed down his coffee cup. "Don't try to tell me it was her idea! Why, Eli? She's pretty, smart, nice. And if you got some kind of erotic charge from being secretive, get over it. I already knew you had a girlfriend."

"You did not know about her," I said, stung.

"I knew a long time ago." At my skeptical look, he added, "Listen, I was there when you told your first lies about eating your vegetables. How could you think I wouldn't know about her?"

"But I—"

"Last year, March, right?" continued my father. "Mid-month. First time you had sex."

My jaw dropped.

He said, "Anybody who was paying attention would have known. You wandered around grinning to yourself. Pulled out the cell phone every half hour when you were home, which wasn't often. Held yourself differently. Didn't hear what I was saying most of the time. And I'm sure you won't remember it, but you did mention her, a few times, by name." He shrugged.

It felt—so strange to realize my father had observed me that closely. I felt naked. Exposed. It was not comfortable or good.

"I was happy for you," my father went on. "I could tell this was a girl you cared about. A girl who cared about you." A pause. I could almost hear him making a deliberate decision to say what came next. "I was hurt when you didn't bring her home."

Damn him. "You know why I couldn't," I said.

"Do I?"

I grabbed the second chair of the dinette set by its back and pulled it toward me. "You know so much. Don't tell me you didn't know that, too."

"But she needed to hear about your mother. She was in pain about your having been so secretive."

I stared at him. "She told you that?"

"She didn't have to tell me. It was obvious."

"Oh," I said. "Of course. Everything is obvious to you."

He sighed. "It's her right to know, Eli."

"Really? How do you figure that, Dad? How do you figure her rights in this particular situation are more important than mine? In this particular situation that happens to involve *my* mother? And *my* genetic inheritance?"

"In a serious relationship—"

"She's—she *was*—just a girlfriend!"

"You weren't serious about her?"

I was silent. So was he. In the end I said, "I needed a relationship that worked for me. That didn't involve other people. What's so wrong with that?"

"*She's* another person."

"You know what I mean. *Other* other people."

"And you know what I mean."

I did. He meant the same thing Viv had meant last night. But they were both wrong. Why couldn't I choose to be in a relationship but not share some things? Didn't I have a right to privacy? Couldn't—shouldn't—someone who loved you make room to give you privacy when you told her that you needed it? Couldn't she do that without question? Not whine about feeling hurt, feeling excluded? Not pick pick pick at you? Couldn't she—couldn't Viv—understand that it was not about her? That it was not personal?

It was then that my father said what he had been wanting to say all along. Because he, too, didn't understand that it was not about him.

"I knew exactly what Vivian was feeling. You've shut me out, too, Eli. Since Ava went into the nursing home, you won't talk, you won't tell me what you're thinking. You've slammed shut like a jailhouse door. I'd hoped you were at least talking to your girlfriend, but now I see you weren't even doing that.

"Don't you understand—you don't have to do this alone," he said. "If you'd only listen to me . . . Eli, you don't have to go through this alone."

"Yes," I said. "I do."

"But—"

"It's my own goddamned choice," I said. "And, by the way, you're really the wrong person to give lectures on the psychological benefits of trust and the rights of the other person in the relationship. Like you don't have secrets of your own. Like there isn't something important that you won't tell me."

"Eli—"

"Let's talk about who slammed shut like a jailhouse door *first*," I said. "Let's talk about who's got secrets that go way back. Before I got this job, even. Way before, Dad."

"You're talking about Wyatt."

"Feel free to share," I said. "Keeping things to yourself is a sign of lack of trust. Of a dysfunctional relationship. Probably even of mental illness."

"My situation and yours are not the same."

"Oh?"

"You don't understand." He looked away.

I said, "Then this is your chance to help me understand."

I waited a full minute more. Then I turned my back, filled my glass of water again, and drained it.

"See you later," I said, and walked out of the kitchen.

CHAPTER 17

I WENT TO WORK.

There was no necessity for it. I wasn't on animal care that weekend; Larry and Mary Alice had thoughtfully given me a couple of regular workweeks before putting me on a rotation that included weekends. Who'd have believed that if I had had the phone number of the woman who was caring for the rabbits on this beautiful spring day, I'd have happily swapped with her?

Then I realized I could go to work anyway. I had an ID badge, I had a card key for our lab, there was other work I could find to do, and why not just go there? The thought was a big relief.

Wyatt Transgenics felt strange and empty at noon on a Sunday. Of course, there were always people in the building—far fewer on weekends, but the security guards were there, and lab assistants like me to care for the animals. Also, some of the scientists worked hours that were anything but regular. The empty feeling simply came from the contrast of the bright May warmth outside to the artificial light of the corridors within. That, and the quiet.

Even knowing that, the building had a creepy feel. I was unable to stop myself from stealing a glance behind me after I signed in with the guard at the front desk. I found my steps speeding up as I mounted the double-helix staircase and passed down the lengths of the carpeted hallways. When I keyed open the door of my own lab and closed it behind me, I felt as if I'd barely made it to safety in time. I rolled my eyes at the poster of Swampy on the wall. I was being ridiculous. But the lab did feel like a refuge.

I pulled out my cell phone and checked for messages. Nothing. There'd been nothing on email, either. Well, that was good. I didn't want Viv rethinking our breakup, or trying to rehash things. There was no point to that.

What I wanted was to work.

I was planning to modify our research database. I'd figured out that if I added a couple of cells to the data matrix, I could calculate some aggregated rabbit milk quantity and quality information that Larry had said would be helpful to have. I sat down at the computer, made a copy of the database to experiment with, and started to play with the data cells and calculations.

But I couldn't concentrate. The silence felt oppressive. I turned on the radio, but even that didn't help—I could feel the building's silence behind the music and the chat. Finally, I went into the next room to visit the rabbits.

They'd already been fed, milked, weighed, their cages

cleaned, their data entered into the logs. I wandered the rows, looking at them as they slept or sat. They were housed in large cages, in social units. I paused by one cage that held Cotton-tail 9, Gloria 4, and Foo-foo 14. Foo-foo 14, a New Zealand White, blinked pinkly at me, her whiskers twitching, her expression seemingly quizzical. I found myself unhooking the cage and reaching in for her. She was warm and soft and cuddled down comfortably in my arms. I refastened the cage and stroked her silky head.

The rabbits were very valuable experimental subjects. They were treated well, but one was not supposed to confuse them with pets. That was an emotional line that you shouldn't cross. Still . . . I'd seen Mary Alice petting the rabbits last week, cooing at them. And I didn't see how it would hurt the experiment for Foo-foo 14 to keep me company on a Sunday afternoon.

No one would know, anyway.

I took the rabbit back into the office area and sat down again at the computer, placing her on my lap. In between staring at the data matrix and typing things on the keyboard, I could reach down from time to time and pet her as she snoozed. It was soothing and it helped me to think. From time to time, too, I looked at my cell phone. But I didn't call anyone, and nobody called me, and after a while I became completely absorbed in mapping the right formulas onto my new data cells and testing my results. Just as I finished fixing an error, I realized my throat was completely dry. Not a big problem; I'd just go to the vending machines for a Coke.

My mistake was taking Foo-foo with me. I didn't think twice, to be honest. She'd been such a cuddly, trouble-free pile of sleepy fur, and I knew we'd be right back in front of the computer within a minute or two. I tucked her in the crook of my arm and let myself out of the lab. Down the hall in front of the soda machine, I fumbled in my pocket for some change, inserted the right amount, and leaned over to grab the can of soda when it descended. Which it did, with the usual clatter.

Only then did I understand that I should have kept both hands on the rabbit.

Foo-foo—valuable Foo-foo, with umpteen generations of genetically engineered rabbit ancestors behind her and a protein in her milk that might potentially save human lives—startled right out of the crook of my arm and bolted down the empty carpeted hall as if there were twenty greyhounds at her heels.

It took me just a second to regroup, but it was a second too long. Foo-foo's flanks disappeared as she loped around the corner to the left.

The next few minutes were like a scene from a bad comedy. "Stop, Foo-foo, stop!" I yelled. I was aware as the words roared out of my throat that they were possibly the most senseless I'd ever spoken.

I sprinted after her.

Only that morning, I'd prided myself on my running prowess, but I had nothing on Foo-foo, and—or so it seemed to me during those endless minutes of pursuit—she took a certain delight in taunting me. How else to explain that she was nearly always in sight, down those long, gray labyrinthine corridors? She'd race down the length of one, me in hot pursuit, and then she'd pause for a few seconds at the end, nose twitching, as if deciding which way to go.

We went left. We went right. We went left again. We went all the way around the building through those empty corridors—and now I was grateful for them; the last thing I wanted was for someone to find out how stupid I'd been. Once I even came within lunging grasp of Foo-foo as she stood sniffing the edge of the wall outside a lab labeled "Robert Judson, PhD." But as my fingertips grazed her fur, she leaped again into the race and, helplessly, so did I.

Then she went in the direction I'd been dreading: into the central corridor that would inevitably take her to the mezzanine and the main staircase above the reception area. I did not wail aloud, "Foo-foo, no!" I only wanted to.

I slowed my steps. If I was lucky, the security guard below wouldn't look up and notice a rabbit loping by above his head. But I personally couldn't afford to be seen running. Instead, I prayed that Foo-foo would still be in sight on the other side of the mezzanine, in the corridor, after I'd crossed the open staircase area. I also prayed she wouldn't decide to hop down the double-helix stairs.

My luck held. I didn't see Foo-foo hopping downstairs, I saw no flashes of fur in the reception area, and the security guard's head remained lowered as he read the newspaper. And, on the other side of the mezzanine, I finally saw Foo-foo at the far end of the corridor, tail to me.

I sped up. Predictably, Foo-foo whipped left, past the sign that said "Human Resources," into a dark, narrow little hallway I'd never noticed before, but which—as I rounded the corner—I saw was a cul-de-sac, with two closed office doors and no way out.

Foo-foo was facing one of the closed office doors. She flirted her tail at me. I approached warily, leaning forward, swaying from side to side as if I were playing goalie in a hockey game. "Foo-foo," I crooned. "Foo-foo . . ."

The office door on the right opened. Foo-foo darted in, and someone inside—a feminine someone—screamed.

It was all over for me then; I wouldn't be able to keep this incident a secret. But at least the rabbit was firmly cornered—I hoped. "Foo-foo," I said aloud again, to give warning of my approach. I dove through the open door right past the woman who'd yelped and into the office—

Except it wasn't an office. It was a small private elevator, and I barely stopped moving in time not to hit its far wall. Foo-foo was crouched up against that wall, trembling. I reached down and scooped her up—and saw, with embarrassment, that she'd left a couple of pellets behind. ·

"Sorry," I said, over my shoulder. "I'm so sorry. She escaped. But she's just a rabbit; she'll be fine, and you don't have to worry, I've got her now. And I'll clean up—"

I turned to face a startled, gape-jawed Judith Ryan. She was clutching a couple of big plastic bags that said "Gap Kids."

There was one of those awful elongated silent moments.

Then I said stupidly: "Oh, it's you. Hi."

She stared at me. Her lip curled. Then she pointed one long white finger. "Get. Out. Of. Here."

"Sure," I said, but just at that moment the elevator door—a single steel electronic door positioned behind the regular wooden door that had made me think this was an office—started to slide shut. I lunged for the extensive control panel and managed to find and push the button that reopened the door. "Sorry," I said again. "Don't you want me to, um, clean—"

"Get. Out."

I tightened my hold on Foo-foo and Got Out, relieved that this was all there was to it.

But I couldn't kid myself. As I trudged back to my part of the building, rabbit held firmly, I realized that there was a good chance I'd be fired as soon as Judith Ryan made the whole incident known.

Great.

CHAPTER 18

I CONFESSED TO Foo-foo's escape promptly on Monday morning but, apart from giving me the expected lecture on not treating the animals as pets, neither Mary Alice nor Larry seemed worried. "It won't happen again," I promised earnestly, and Mary Alice replied, "We believe you, Eli. Now, take it easy, and show us those database modifications."

Larry was already leaning over the computer, but he looked up at my face, grinned, and added, "Although I have to say that I really, really wish I'd seen you chasing Foo-foo through the building."

"Judith Ryan from Human Resources might call," I began, as a picture of her rigid face flashed into my mind.

Mary Alice waved her hand dismissively. "HR is about paperwork. They have no real power. Larry's your boss. And, for crying out loud, Wyatt himself hired you, right?"

"Yes, but Judith Ryan—" I could just see her in that elevator, glaring at me.

"He's so young and naïve, it hurts," said Larry to Mary Alice. He turned to me. "Don't worry about it, Eli. Nobody's going to make you stay after school. You messed up; you fixed it; you told your boss; case closed. Hey, I'll even write you a recommendation someday and I won't say a word about you chasing white rabbits." He chuckled. "All right, kid?"

"All right," I said. But still, I jumped every time the lab phone rang that day, and the next, and the next, expecting—something. Some repercussion.

Rationally, I did understand what Larry had said. Foo-foo's escape was a mistake on my part, but not an unforgivable one and not a big deal. More important things probably happened a hundred times a day at Wyatt Transgenics.

But to me the incident had somehow felt significant. Was that just because, as Larry said, I was young and naïve and didn't understand the adult work world? Was I really still expecting to be publicly reprimanded for the slightest transgression?

I replayed that final sequence from the chase in my mind. Cornering Foo-foo in that dark corridor. One of the wooden doors suddenly opening outward. Foo-foo's dash through that doorway. Judith Ryan's scream. My own fast lunge into the little elevator—

Wait. That was it. That was what was bugging me. Wasn't it a little peculiar, putting an elevator behind a regular wooden office door? The other elevators in the building looked like elevators. They had sliding steel doors that weren't concealed by anything. They had push buttons outside.

Foo-foo hadn't discovered a small elevator. Foo-foo had discovered a *hidden* elevator.

Or not. Maybe I was being melodramatic. Maybe it was a *private* elevator. Why shouldn't there be a private elevator in a big building where important work was done? Probably it was desirable for some people—politicians, visiting scientists—to tour Wyatt Transgenics quietly, bypassing the public entries and corridors. Maybe there was even more than one private elevator or corridor in such a big, specialized building. The more I thought about that, the less strange it seemed. And, I reflected, if it really bothered me, I could always ask Dr. Wyatt himself. "I noticed this private elevator over in the HR wing. What's that for?"

Yes, I could imagine myself asking him that question. Casually. I really could.

But I could also imagine him staring at me incredulously and replying with the obvious. "So people can move between floors without other people staring at them, when necessary."

With that, the whole incident did truly seem trivial. More rabbit-chasing. It wasn't like I didn't have other things, important things, to think about.

One of those things, of course, was Viv. I missed her. I missed her every day as the week passed. A thousand times in my mind I reached for the phone to call her; ten thousand times I imagined her with me. Once, on Thursday, I saw on my cell phone's message log that she'd called—her phone number flashed up at me as if the digits were in red—and my heart jumped. But she'd hung up without leaving a message. I thought about calling her back, but I turned off the phone instead and put it away.

Because, as much as I missed her—all right, longed for her—I couldn't imagine being with Viv now. Not with her knowing about my mother . . . not with her looking at me with that knowledge, that pity, in her eyes.

The need for distraction pulled at me. The long empty weekend ahead haunted me. I wasn't tied to Viv anymore. There was no need to feel disloyal.

So, on Friday morning I called Kayla Matheson and asked her to play tennis with me that evening. She said yes, promptly, and—unlike Viv—hung up without extraneous chat. That night, I left work on time, with everybody else. I was glad, so glad, to have plans. Plans that, if I was lucky, wouldn't involve much talk.

Kayla and I had arranged to meet promptly at six on the Cambridge public courts, located not far from Dr. Wyatt's big house. The moment I saw her—in another minuscule white tennis dress, this one with a square neck that exposed the line of her neck and shoulders—I couldn't believe that I hadn't been able to remember exactly how she looked. How she moved. How she . . .

"We're over on the second court," she said cheerfully. "Are you ready?"

"Yeah," I said. "You want first serve?"

"Sure."

I stood back by the baseline, liking her for not wasting any time chatting. She smiled and then got a charming, serious expression on her face as she gripped her racket and prepared to toss the ball into the air with her left hand.

This really could be fun, I realized suddenly. Kayla looked good. She was clearly athletic. We'd have a nice rally. I'd go easy; keep the ball in play—

Kayla's serve exploded from her racket like a rocket. I could not have returned it if I'd tried. "One–love!" she called a second later. And she grinned.

Our eyes met and held. I knew she saw how shocked I was. Finally, I nodded. I felt a smile of my own pulling at the corners of my mouth and I let it happen. Kayla laughed.

I jogged away to retrieve the ball. I lobbed it back to her, to where she was now standing, close to the net. "Okay," I said. "I'm really ready now. I won't underestimate you again."

"Good," she said seriously, and moved to serve.

I backed up. Her serve came smashing down again, but this time I expected it. I slammed it cross-court, near the net, but she was there, with a backhand shot that angled the ball forcefully behind where I was, so that I had to race to return it— and she was already at the net, leaping into the air to intercept the ball and dink it, with the merest calculated flick of her strong right wrist, so that it landed just barely over the net on my side.

"Two–love," Kayla said demurely. "Hey, I thought you said you could play. I thought you said you would stop underestimating me." Her eyes were dancing now, with glee, with triumph. "I play varsity in college, you know."

And then I was the one laughing aloud. "I didn't know," I said. "Well, serve again—and may God help me."

"He's not interested," said Kayla smartly.

That serve of hers again.

She beat me, in the end, 6–3, 4–6, 7–6, and by the end of the game, I trusted her physicality, her command of her body, completely. It was incredible. I'd never known anything like it. I'd never known anyone like her.

By the end of the game, I was barely holding back at all . . . and maybe I didn't have to. Maybe, with her—here on the tennis court, if nowhere else—I could let go for a short time and just be myself. Without carefulness. Without . . . and here came a strange nugget of truth.

Without fear.

CHAPTER 19

BUT TO MY SURPRISE and chagrin, that night, I still missed Viv. I longed for her fiercely, more even than before. I didn't understand it. I had had a wonderful time with Kayla, and we had plans to meet again in the morning for breakfast at Dr. Wyatt's, followed by more tennis. I'd thought, defiantly, that I might even skip going to visit my mother later in the day. Kayla could distract me the way I needed to be distracted; she was so perfect. I was sure of it.

And yet, as I lay in bed, all I could think about was Viv. I'd close my eyes and try to drift off to sleep, and then I'd find myself reaching out for her. I'd fix an image of Kayla, beautiful Kayla, in my mind, try to focus on it . . . and there again, instead, would be Viv. Ordinary, well-known, earnest, outspoken, unathletic, emotionally demanding Viv.

The way she'd take my hand and tilt her head to the side and slide a glance at me, a smile tugging at the corner of her mouth. Her giggle. And how quiet she'd get, how serious, almost solemn . . .

Okay. I wanted her, yes. Still. You don't rip somebody out of yourself that quickly, that easily. She was the first girl I'd loved, after all, and she'd loved me, too, even though she'd known me, truly, so little. She'd been sincere, and I knew that. It—she—was valuable to me. So I understood why I kept on wanting her despite the fact of how things were going to be— had to be—now. My body was operating blindly, habitually, in the same way that a human brain could still receive phantom, lying signals from an amputated hand or foot.

What I didn't understand, though, was why I kept talking to her in my head. Arguing with her. Justifying myself. Growing angrier and angrier. . . . How could she want so much? How could she presume—why couldn't she just have done what I wanted, because I wanted it? Couldn't she understand that I knew what was best for me, knew the best way to handle things for myself? That I needed things to be a certain way in order to survive? So that I could get up every day and do what I had to do? So I could just go on?

Her and her damned sharing. Her and her damned trust. Yeah, that all worked fine, maybe . . . when you were dealing with the ordinary stuff of life.

Real trust would have had her giving me what I needed. Not prying; accepting. Accepting blindly, if necessary—and it was.

But she wasn't capable of that.

Another thing that made me angry was that I suspected I knew what Viv had been up to this last week. I suspected she'd spent all her free time researching Huntington's disease. Toting books home from the library to read. Surfing the web. Reading Internet chat and list discussions about HD. Thinking. Putting together patterns with me in the middle of them. Trying to figure me—it—me—out.

Yes, I could almost feel Viv learning about HD, or trying to, from twenty blocks away, and there was no way to make her stop. No way to keep the knowledge from her. And if she were to call my father—he'd talk to her now. Oh, yes, he'd talk freely.

So, if Viv wanted to know where my mother was, she would find out. She could even—there was a stubbornness to Viv—go to the nursing home herself. Go to see for herself.

Please God, no.

And all at once I understood that *this* was why I'd been thinking about not going to see my mother. About hanging out with Kayla instead. It was just in case Viv showed up, informed by my father about my regular time to visit.

More than that, actually. I didn't want to go today because Viv might have been there at any time this past week. Might have met my mother. Might have trespassed. And if I learned that she had gone there . . . if a nurse or attendant said anything to me about that . . .

I could feel rage—and fear, but mostly rage—threaten to fountain up inside me. Viv might have seen my mother in that wheelchair, her face vacant, and thought—wrongly—that she understood. Thought she understood her. Thought she understood me.

But the woman called Ava Samuels, the one who existed in

that nursing home today, as the end approached—she could not give Viv the slightest picture of who she once had been. Of the two—at least two—women she had been before.

Ava Louise Lange Samuels. Brilliant economist, professor at the Harvard Business School. Picture-perfect wife and mother . . . but with an abnormally long trinucleotide repeat in a particular dominant gene, hidden deep in her DNA where nobody could see it or know about it. Not her husband or her son. Not even Ava herself, or her doctor—at least, not without the testing that had only been available publicly since 1993.

And you had to already be suspicious to do the testing anyway.

The trinucleotide: Cytosine-Adenine-Guanine. C-A-G. A normal sequence. Even to have repeats was absolutely normal. Eleven repeats was in the normal range. So, in fact, was twenty, thirty, forty. The human genome could tolerate a lot of variation. Variation was good, normal, healthy. To a point.

But if you happened to have more than forty repeats of C-A-G at the tip of chromosome four, then you were carrying the HD time bomb, set to go off—well, no one could say exactly when. In middle age sometime, usually.

That was what happened to my mother. Bit by bit, she started acting oddly.

But what's odd? Suppose, at age thirty-two, you stumbled while you walked. Suppose, at age forty, you threw a plate at your husband's head. Maybe you were just being ordinarily clumsy. Maybe you had been provoked beyond bearing. People without HD did those things all the time. Maybe it was nothing.

But maybe it was the beginning. Maybe it wasn't you doing those things. Maybe it was the trinucleotide repeats . . . going to work on you. Starting to eat away at who you were. To mutate and possess your very self.

Destiny was written in the trinucleotide repeats. That was what I knew, what Viv could never know, no matter how much research she might do. The words *progressive insanity* didn't even begin to cover it.

C-A-G-C-A-G-C-A-G-C-A-G-C-A-G-C-A-G-C-A-G-C-A-
G-C-A-G-C-A-G-C-A-G-C-A-G-C-A-G-C-A-G-C-A-G-C-A-
G-C-A-G-C-A-G-C-A-G-C-A-G-C-A-G-C-A-G-C-A-G-C-A-
G-C-A-G-C-A-G-C-A-G-C-A-G-C-A-G-C-A-G-C-A-G-C-A-
G-C-A-G-C-A-G-C-A-G-C-A-G-C-A-G-C-A-G-C-A-G-C-A-
G-C-A-G-C-A-G-C-A-G-C-A-G-C-A-G-C-A-G-C-A-G-C-A-
G-C-A-G-C-A-G-C-A-G-C-A-G-C-A-G-C-A-G-C-A-G.

Viv could look and look at my mother, quiet and docile these days, as death approached. And Viv could read and read. But she couldn't know, couldn't know, couldn't know.

Too many C-A-G repeats at the tip of chromosome four.

Viv couldn't know what it had been like for me and my father. There was no way to describe those years in which Ava Louise Lange Samuels lived with us, out of control, turning into a different person, going insane day by day—and knowing it.

As I would know it.

Yes, much as I longed for Viv, it was good that she wasn't with me right now. Because if she had been, and I'd felt what I felt now, this confusion and hate and rage and misery—

Somewhere in me, I realized, I needed someone to lash out

at. This was why I attacked my father verbally, emotionally, every way I could. Viv had only been safe when she was in her little compartment, separated from the more horrible things in my life. And if she wouldn't stay there, wouldn't stay safe in the compartment, then I might not be able to trust myself. She wouldn't be safe from me. Because I wanted—I needed—someone to blame—

I took several deep breaths.

I needed things to be the way they had been. But they couldn't be.

Kayla, I told myself. Think of Kayla.

But I couldn't soothe myself, couldn't forget Viv. Not yet, anyway. And so I gave up. I turned on the bedside lamp. It was just after two a.m. I prowled into the kitchen and made coffee. Then I pulled out a Terry Pratchett novel to read. Corporal Carrot—Viv's favorite character. Sitting up at the kitchen table, I read his adventures doggedly for the rest of the night.

When dawn came and the sun climbed into the sky, I got dressed and—with relief—went to meet Kayla and Dr. Wyatt for breakfast.

CHAPTER 20

It FELT MORE than a little strange to sit idle and watch Dr. Wyatt cook. He refused outright to let Kayla or me help. Instead, he gave us coffee and sat us on the other side of the kitchen island from the stove, and I watched in surprise as he calmly managed three pans with order and efficiency. In no time, a neat platter of French toast, a pile of perfectly crisp bacon, and a shallow bowl of scrambled eggs were ready to be placed on the table on the sunporch, where croissants, grapes and blackberries, china place settings, linen napkins, and more coffee awaited.

"I'm impressed," I said to Dr. Wyatt as I pulled out a chair for Kayla. She brushed against me for a millisecond as she moved to sit, and I caught the fresh light scent of her shampoo. I again felt filled with amazement at her beauty, and with gratification at her clear interest in me. In fact, when she'd greeted me earlier, she'd displayed a demure downcast to her eyes—coupled with a sudden flashing glance upward—that made me feel ready to forget everything else in the world but her. We'd be alone later. I looked down at the top of her head, at the sweet jut of her cheekbone, the curve of her bare downy shoulder in her summer dress. I could kiss her if I wanted, later. I suddenly knew that, knew it with complete certainty. She'd like it; she even expected it. I could touch her and—

I grabbed my own seat and sat.

Dr. Wyatt was seated, too, and had already reached for the eggs. "What, Eli, you didn't think I could use a stove? Set a table? Expected we'd be ordering bagels from the place around the corner?"

"Well . . . you did mention the other day that you had a cook," I said. My brain was racing ahead on the other track, however. Kayla was going to be a sophomore in college. She wouldn't be a virgin like Viv had been . . . and I wasn't one now, either, for that matter. It would be totally different—no strings, no emotional entanglements. And the way Kayla had moved in her body when she played tennis . . . I'd been lying to myself, all at once I knew that. Pretending I hadn't been thinking about this all along, from the second I saw Kayla. Maybe breaking up with Viv had nothing to do with her prying and snooping, her emotional demands, nothing to do with HD. Maybe it was all just normal hormones . . . time to move on, to experiment . . . why be tied down when you were only eighteen? Viv was far too intense anyway.

"Eli? French toast?"

"Oh—yes, sure." I managed to accept the platter that Dr. Wyatt passed to me. He was continuing the conversation like a civilized person. I tried hard to tune in again.

"The truth is I'm limited to cooking breakfast things," he said. "But only from choice. Cooking is a skill very close to chemistry, you know—and though I didn't major in it, I took a lot of chem as an undergraduate. I don't think it's wise for scientists to specialize too quickly. Nowadays, especially, we understand that things connect in all sorts of unpredictable ways. The race goes to the prepared. Remember that next year, Eli, when you start college. I approve of double-majors, by the way. I only wish Kayla had at least—"

"You know that I would never make a good scientist," Kayla said calmly. "My parents reconciled themselves to that, and so should you."

"Maybe you weren't meant to end up doing scientific research," Dr. Wyatt conceded. "It bored you so much that summer. But you're so smart, Kayla, and to spend all your time reading eighteenth-century novels—I simply fail to see the utility of it."

"I'm supposed to be the one figuring out utility, not you." Kayla didn't seem to have taken offense; she was smiling fondly at Dr. Wyatt. "Trust me, Q. I'll be fine."

Hearing Dr. Wyatt called Q helped retrieve me from my sexual haze. I had heard Kayla use it before, but it still struck me as off-key—as strange as if the prophet Mohammed had materialized in the room and Kayla had greeted him with "Hey, Mo!" It made me remember, anew, that Kayla was more than a beautiful face and body. That she, too, had a history and a mind and was bound to be complicated and full of unknowns.

This thought abruptly cooled me off.

I dug into my French toast. "How's it going with your internship?" I asked Kayla.

"Oh, so far they have me writing press releases and updating the website. But they also said that I can read the slush in my spare time, if I want to." She leaned forward, shredding a croissant between her fingers. "If I want to! I can't wait!"

"Slush?" I asked.

"The manuscripts that people send in uninvited." She ate the tiniest bit of croissant. "I know most of the slush pile manuscripts are supposed to be just awful, but it seems to me that you never know. There could be an amazing novel in there, or some fascinating nonfiction. It happens."

"Rarely." Dr. Wyatt snorted. "Face it, Kayla: Most people are idiots and everything they do bears that out."

"But sometimes—"

"No, no. I know something about this, because you find it in every field of endeavor. Mark my words: You'll waste the summer looking for treasure in that slush pile, but you won't find it. Just like, back when I used to teach, I'd look and look for signs of real intelligence, real originality, real thought, in my students' work, but most of the time it just wasn't there. The best you could get was a dull combination of memorization and regurgitation. Like from a clever monkey." A look of distaste passed over his face, and then he shrugged. "Of course, that's a useful lesson, too. You might as well learn it now, Kayla. It will save you time in the long run. Teach you not to waste time on fools."

"You're so cynical!" said Kayla.

"No," Dr. Wyatt said mildly. "I'm realistic." He turned to

me. "Be honest, Eli. Haven't you found what I say to be the case, in the admittedly short time you've been on this earth? Aren't most people unable to string a logical thought together, unable to express themselves coherently, unable to do much of anything with competence and clarity—let alone with originality?"

I hesitated. Secretly, I had sometimes had similar thoughts about a lot of my classmates. And about teachers, too, to be truthful. I'd been impatient sometimes, when people seemed particularly clueless. But I didn't feel that way about everybody. And I didn't quite know what Dr. Wyatt was driving at. Or why he was suddenly watching me so closely, with such intensity. It made me feel uncomfortable. I wanted to say something to please him, but I wasn't sure what it would be. Wouldn't just agreeing with him be—well, monkeylike? Especially since I really didn't know what I thought?

"The people I've been working with at Wyatt Transgenics seem very smart," I temporized. "Larry Donohue and Mary Alice Gregorian."

Dr. Wyatt made a sweeping-away motion with one hand. His eyes were very bright, suddenly. "People who have skills that you don't have often seem smart at first," he said. "It doesn't mean anything. Think beyond that. Think more broadly. How often are you genuinely impressed with someone? Tell me the truth. How often do you think, *This person is superior to me*?"

After what felt like a pause that went on too long, I shook my head. "I don't know if I've *ever* thought that, exactly, but—"

"You have never thought anyone was superior to you."

I felt as if I were suddenly standing on ground that was about to crumble beneath my feet. He'd twisted my words around. That was not what I'd said. "Well, I think *you* are superior to me!" I retorted. "Obviously."

He didn't say anything, but he liked that; I could tell. Reassured, I went on. "Dr. Wyatt, listen, I haven't really thought much about this. But I know that it doesn't matter if I'm better at some things than other people are. That just makes sense. People have different talents. People contribute different things to the world. Like . . . I'm not musical. I have nothing to give to anybody there. Somebody else has to give to me. You hear what I'm saying?"

There was a long, long pause. Then: "Oh, yes," said Dr. Wyatt softly. "I hear you, Eli. I hear you quite plainly. I also hear that you lied a minute ago. You *have* thought about this. You've thought about it quite often, I judge. You've thought quite often about superiority. And—given your mother's situation—no doubt you've thought a lot about genetics and destiny as well. The way that genetics enforces one's destiny. The way that one cannot escape. Am I right?"

I was unable to speak. Unable to move.

"Of course I'm right," said Dr. Wyatt. He smiled cheerily. "More eggs?"

CHAPTER 21

I DID NOT STAY, after all, to play tennis with Kayla. As soon as breakfast was over, I said bluntly that I had to go; I had to visit my mother at the nursing home. I looked Dr. Wyatt in the eye as I said it. Then I turned to Kayla and said, "My mother has a genetic disease called Huntington's. It causes mental and physical deterioration and eventually insanity, beginning sometime in middle age. It can't be treated or cured."

One or both of them began to say something, but I didn't listen. I walked as rapidly as I could out of Dr. Wyatt's house and down the street and around the corner, and there I found a bush and threw up behind it.

Genetics enforces one's destiny. One cannot escape.

You've thought quite often about superiority.

As I straightened, I caught the eye of a little boy—perhaps five or six years old—who was standing in the small front yard of a nearby house. The child moved forward a few steps and stared down with great interest. "Puke!" he said.

"Sorry," I said. "Look, if you'd like to go tell your parents, maybe they'll have something I can clean it up with. Uh—a shovel, maybe. And a garbage bag."

The boy turned and ran inside his house. I felt jumpy, odd, nervous—wanting to leave but also feeling fixed to the spot because of the child. A couple of minutes later the boy reemerged, still alone, but holding a red plastic toy shovel and a folded plastic trash bag. I had him hold open the bag for me while I cleaned up. Together, we tied off the trash bag and deposited it in a barrel.

"There," I said. I squatted and looked the boy in the eye. "Thanks," I said.

"After you puke, you feel better," said the child wisely.

"Right," I said. "Bye now, kid. And thanks."

"Bye now, man." The boy was smiling at me sunnily. "Come back sometime. We can play." He held out his hand, and I took it and we shook, gently.

I got up, feeling his gaze still on me, feeling his longing that I would stay and play. For a moment, I wished I could. I did think about going up to the house to find the boy's parents or guardians, whoever. They needed to understand that any jerk who came by and puked could be this kid's friend for life. It was a dangerous world; adults were supposed to protect their children, and these folks were not being watchful.

But I didn't have the strength to go talk to adults right now. So instead I said pedantically to the boy, "Now, remember, you really shouldn't talk to or play with strangers like me. Haven't your parents told you that?"

The hero-worship faded from the boy's face and was replaced

by a kind of betrayal. And a scowl. He nodded. He backed away from me until he reached the safety of his front steps.

I felt sick again but I didn't know, either, what else I could have said or done. So much for superiority.

I trudged to the nearest subway station and waited on the platform for a long time for a train. I kept thinking about the little boy . . . and then, all at once, I was aware that I wanted my mother. Not really, of course . . . not that woman in the nursing home. But . . . my mother. The mother she'd been when I was five or six.

The feeling filled me, and I let the next train come and go, and then went around the platform to the other side, and without thinking or planning, went in the other direction, away from home, toward the nursing home, a couple of hours before I was due there.

Maybe it was encountering the little boy. Or maybe, sub-consciously, I wanted to make true the lie I had told Dr. Wyatt and Kayla. Or—maybe—it was something more mysterious. In any event, I was there by eleven o'clock, and the moment I walked into my mother's room, and saw my father sitting by her bedside, I knew why I was there. It was happening at last, and I—I had come to bear witness, to be with my father, and to say good-bye.

I watched the back of my father's head for a time. My mother was lying still for once, eyes closed. Sleeping, perhaps. I hoped. Finally I said, "Hey," softly. I knew, somehow, that my father knew I was there.

And maybe—wasn't it possible?—my mother did, too.

My father moved his head, but didn't really turn. "I've been calling your cell phone," he said.

"I had it off," I said. "I'm sorry." And I was. After a moment my father nodded, and with his foot pulled the second chair closer.

"Sit," he said. "It's almost time."

I sat next to him and I looked at my mother's face, and then at my father's impassive one, and we waited.

It wasn't a surprise, of course. We—my father and I—had been told a while ago that my mother was nearing the end of her life. She couldn't talk anymore, in any way. The wild, uncontrollable flailing of her arms and legs, which had embarrassed her so hugely, which had been so scary and dangerous to her and to others, had quieted down to shivers and shakes. "A few weeks, at most," the doctor had said. But he had said it months ago, last fall, and she had hung on, and somehow . . . somehow I had put it out of my mind. And now it was time.

You could feel it, in the room with us. Death.

I was choked with fear.

Nonetheless, I moved to the other side of the bed and took my mother's other hand in mine, feeling how it trembled. And then my father reached out across the bed and we held hands. He was trembling along with her. So was I.

Then, quietly, though she had not been quiet in many, many years, my mother simply was no more. I cannot describe it except to say that there is no mistaking the sudden emptiness. There is no mistaking that moment of change.

Dr. Wyatt had proclaimed to me that there was really no such thing as the individual human consciousness, no mysterious "something" or essence that made a human a human. And only a few minutes ago, I would have sworn that there was really nothing left of the person who had been Ava Louise Lange Samuels, even though she was still alive.

But—now that she actually had died, I could feel the difference. Something had changed. Something had departed. Something—someone—was now missing from the world. Viv would call it a soul. I—I didn't know what to call it. I only knew it had been there, and was no longer.

I heard my father exhale. His fingers tightened on mine, and I returned his grip. I didn't look up, though. I closed my eyes. I lifted my mother's hand to my cheek. Just for a second. Then I put it back down on the bed, by her side.

CHAPTER 22

I TOOK THE FOLLOWING few days off from work, not because I wanted to—it would have been a relief to have something concrete and impersonal to do for hours every day—but because my father asked. My mother had long ago signed a form to donate her body to scientific research, so there wasn't to be an actual funeral, but a memorial service was scheduled for Thursday morning, at a chapel at the Harvard Business School. Many of my mother's old colleagues and friends would want to come, my father said. My mother had been very impressive, and very admired, once.

"I know," I said. It was the day before the memorial service, and we were walking by the river.

"Do you?" said my father.

"Yes."

"I wonder. She was an extraordinary person. Just—uncommon. Her life wasn't all tragic. There are many things to celebrate about it."

"I know."

"I'm not sure you do. I think there's no way you really can know. You won't let yourself. That's what I most regret, I think."

I contained my impatience. My father's backward-tending musings seemed to me to accomplish nothing, though I knew I had to be there to hear them since that was what he wanted. That was okay. Just so long as I didn't have to cough up similar thoughts. I didn't have any. I didn't want to look back. I couldn't understand why he hadn't used up all these thoughts long, long ago.

In many ways my mother had been dead for years, hadn't she? And all these friends and colleagues who were supposedly going to celebrate her life tomorrow—I hadn't noticed them visiting her these last years. Or even calling us, or providing support to my father in any way.

He had been—we had been—alone.

But I wasn't going to get enraged about that now. There was just no point. It was over. I felt my pace speed up a little anyway. I couldn't help it. But after a few seconds, I adjusted it back down so that my steps matched my father's again.

And we plodded on.

We'd been taking long walks together every day. I wasn't sure that my father found my presence a comfort—we continued uneasy with each other, and I kept my thoughts to myself—but he kept asking me to come out, and of course I did. We would walk and walk, and occasionally my father would make pointless comments like the ones he'd just made. And other times I would say, "Dad? Are you okay?" and he would say, "Fine, and you, Eli?" and I would say, "Fine."

We did not talk about the future—our future, and how things would now change—though I was aware that that conversation would have to occur. I wanted it to. After the service, maybe, he would speak up. I wondered if he would be honest with me about our financial situation. About the debt that, surely, there'd be some hope of overcoming now that there wouldn't be any new bills. I wondered if he would be thinking about dating other women—of remarrying, even. His whole life could change, if he wanted.

He was free. Did it matter to him? Had he realized it yet? He must have. He must have been longing for this for years. Why couldn't he say so? Did he think I wouldn't know? Wouldn't expect it? Wouldn't understand?

Did he think I was selfish enough not to want freedom for him?

I ventured a glance at him as we trudged. His face, in profile, was down-turned, unreadable. He was fifty-two years old. He had thrown so much of his life away. Was he planning to salvage what was left? To indulge, finally, in wine, women, and song? He deserved all of that. He'd been good to her. To me. He could have a full life now, a new life. He ought to want it.

But, as far as I could tell, he was still stuck dwelling on the past.

She was an extraordinary person.

So what? Who cared? She'd caused devastation and destruction. She'd wrecked lives, mostly his. Mine, too, maybe—if . . .

if I had HD. She hadn't meant to do that, of course. But she had, all the same.

Well. One thing I knew. I could make sure that my father didn't have any additional burdens, any additional debt, any additional heartache, any additional life wreckage. Enough was enough. I was eighteen, and employed. In every way, I could take care of myself now. I could move on, and in doing that, force him to do it, too.

I could even take the HD test and—if necessary—lie to him about the results. Why hadn't that occurred to me before? I could even *not* take the test, but tell him I had. I could easily mock up a letter like the one he'd gotten. I could help free him from that last anxiety. I could free him of me. I could free him, and he could forget any of it had ever happened. He could move on and not throw any more of his life away. Not on her. Not on me.

The only problem was that I couldn't quite imagine talking to him openly about his new freedom. He would have to start the conversation if it were to occur.

Or I could just go ahead and do what I had to do, without speaking of it to him.

We walked on. Then, as we rounded a curve in the path, the glass-and-brick cathedral that was Wyatt Transgenics loomed ahead. It dominated the landscape. This was the first time we'd come this way on our walks.

"I assume you haven't invited that man to the memorial service," said my father sharply.

We both knew who he meant. "No," I said. It hadn't even occurred to me to invite Dr. Wyatt. I had not seen or communicated with Dr. Wyatt since the breakfast on the morning my mother died—a morning that now seemed as if it had happened a long time ago. I remembered the strange twist of that conversation, but I also knew that I had overreacted to it. After the service, I would call and apologize. I needed my job, liked it—as well as the career opportunities it offered. And there were still questions to be answered about Dr. Wyatt and his history with my parents. I still wanted answers . . . didn't I? Even with my mother dead.

Or maybe I didn't. Maybe this, too, didn't matter anymore.

"Because I'd throw him out if he showed up," said my father.

Okay. It still mattered to my father.

I stopped on the path. "Why?" I asked calmly. "Why would you throw him out? Why do you care? Will you tell me now why you hate him so much? It had something to do with her, I know. But now she's dead. Can you let it go? Can you tell me? It can't be important anymore."

He had stopped, too, a few steps ahead of me. He turned back. Our eyes met. And I expected him to say no again, flatly, but he surprised me. He drew in a deep breath, closed his eyes, and then opened them. He said, slowly but clearly: "It's still important. And maybe I will tell you."

I couldn't believe it. "You'll tell me?"

"I might. I'll think about it. That's the best I can do right now, Eli."

I nodded. "Okay. Fair enough." Now it was my turn to pause, and then I used unfair artillery—unfair because, even though I wasn't lying, even though I meant it—I did mean it—I was also saying it to manipulate. I needed to say it, though. Maybe as much as I knew he longed to hear it.

I said, "I love you, Dad."

Now he was the one who was surprised. He glanced away so I couldn't see his face, but I did see the movement in his throat as he swallowed. Then he took a step forward and reached out to grip my hand.

"Me, too, son," he said.

I gripped back. Just for a moment. Then we turned, side by side, and walked on. We didn't look at each other, or at Wyatt Transgenics as it towered above our heads as we passed.

CHAPTER 23

THE EVENING AFTER the memorial service I went running for over an hour, and in the middle of the night I swallowed two sleeping pills, but I still slept badly, full of rage and longing and uncertainty that I kept trying to stamp down. I just wanted to be . . . robotlike. That would work.

Viv again.

She had come to the service. In my memory, I could see her still. She'd entered the chapel with a firm step, but after a single glance across the width of the chapel during which our eyes met, she'd looked quickly away and made a beeline for the last row of chairs. She'd settled, alone, into a seat on the end, and sort of collapsed into herself, ducking her head to study the little folded paper my father had prepared to explain the content of the service. Hymns. Poems. Prayer.

I had not contacted her. I had not asked her to come—but I found I was glad to see her.

She did not raise her head, and so I took the opportunity to watch her, just for a minute. She wore a black blouse and skirt with little white flowers all over it, and, on her head, a small, slightly-battered straw hat. Thrift store, I guessed. But, as so often, Viv had gotten her outfit slightly wrong. This time it was the fabric. It was over ninety degrees outside, and even from across the room—even in the air-conditioning of the chapel—I could see the beads of perspiration on her forehead.

She was wearing high-heeled sandals with thin straps. She'd crossed her legs and one little foot dangled beneath the hem of her long skirt, bare ankle circling nervously. She had slender, sensitive ankles . . .

Her head came up abruptly and she caught me. I nodded to her calmly, as if I hadn't just been ogling—at my dead mother's memorial service, too—mouthed "Thanks for coming," and turned definitely away. Then it was my turn to feel her eyes on me, throughout the entire service. I didn't look at her directly again, though, and when the chapel finally cleared afterward, I discovered that she had not been one of the people who lingered to talk to my father or me. She had left.

I told myself I was glad about that, too. I told myself it was just as well, because Kayla Matheson had come also—slipping in as the service was starting, but staying long enough to briefly wish me sympathy afterward—and I felt uncomfortable when I thought of Viv seeing me with Kayla. But I could have predicted that Viv would leave as quickly as possible, because Viv is proud. I forget that from time to time, but it's true. She had attended my mother's memorial service; she would send a note to me, expressing her sympathy; and in the background she would be reading about HD and brooding—I knew it—but, even if she were dying inside, she would not call me.

Which was fine. Which was good, because my mother's death had not changed anything major in me or my life. At least, not anything that would affect Viv and me.

Knowing that trying to sleep more was useless, I got up at five a.m. and was at work an hour later, entering the accumulated data that had piled up while I was out, and then running reports on it and on last week's data for everybody in the lab. By late afternoon, I had everything that I was responsible for squared away and in control again, and as people began streaming out for the weekend, I heard myself volunteering to take the rabbit-care detail for the next couple of days. That way, the woman who was originally scheduled to do it could go to the Cape with her boyfriend. "Wow, thanks," she said. "I was just complaining about it for the sake of complaining, you know; I didn't really mean—I wasn't asking—"

"It's no problem," I said. "Go have fun, Robin. I'm happy to do it." Which was a fact; I was glad to have rabbit-care plans for the weekend. Any plans.

"Well, thanks. You know I'll do it for you sometime." Robin began scribbling on a Post-it note. "Just in case you have a question or something, let me give you my cell phone number."

"Okay, great." I accepted the piece of paper and stuck it on the frame of my computer monitor.

Hand on the doorknob of the lab, Robin still lingered, looking guilty. But the pull of a weekend at the beach was strong, and I could almost see her thinking that it wasn't as if rabbit-care patrol was difficult, or as if shift-swapping wasn't done all the time. I waited, and she said, "Just, uh, don't let any rabbits out again, you hear?"

That was it, then. "Does everybody know about that?" I asked. I did my best to look and sound upright and responsible. "How embarrassing. Well, believe me, Foo-foo and all her friends are staying in their cages where they belong. And any questions, I'll call you. Deal?"

Robin was reassured. "Deal. Hey, it's not like letting Foo-foo out was so bad. I remember once, this guy fed the wrong nutrients to some mice and ruined a whole experimental cycle." She opened the door. "Aren't you leaving? You have a few hours before the ten p.m. data collection. You can get dinner and then come back."

"I have a few more things to do here first," I said, gesturing vaguely at my computer.

"All right." Finally, she was gone. I sank into my swivel chair and just sat there, feeling the evening gather in around me. I closed my eyes. It was funny how much easier I found it to be alone at the lab than I did at home. How calm I felt now, as, out in the corridors, the footsteps and voices passed by and faded and the building settled down into its after-hours quiet that no longer felt creepy to me.

I sat there for a long time, not even thinking. I might even have dozed off.

When, eventually, I came back into myself, I checked my cell phone for messages. None. I left a message for my father to say I'd be working late. "Really working," I told the recording. "I mean, I'm not having dinner with—I'm taking care of the rabbits." I hung up feeling chagrined—why had I said that? It wasn't my father's business if I saw Dr. Wyatt. I would see Dr. Wyatt if I wanted to.

Though, in fact, I hadn't seen him or talked to him that day, or all week, and although I thought he must surely know about my mother's death, since Kayla Matheson did, he hadn't come with Kayla to the memorial service.

It was just as well, of course. My father might have made good on his threat to throw Dr. Wyatt out if he'd shown up. Maybe Dr. Wyatt had known he wouldn't be welcomed by my father and had kindly stayed away, while sending Kayla.

My father had definitely noticed Kayla. Well, who wouldn't? He'd stared after her as she strode confidently out of the chapel after talking to me. "That girl," he said abruptly to me, later on. He'd described her, meticulously. "A friend of yours?"

"Yes," I'd said cautiously.

"A *new* friend?" he pressed.

"Yes."

The strangest series of expressions had passed over his face. One of them was almost—fear. And then, for a moment, I'd thought he was about to start screaming at me. But in the end, all he'd said was: "You ought to be with that nice girl, that Vivian Fadiman. Where did *she* go?" And he'd turned away.

A shiver shook me, now, in the lab. I got up and adjusted the air-conditioning, but it didn't help. All at once I was overwhelmingly conscious of the unanswered questions that I'd mostly refused to think about these past weeks. Why was Dr. Wyatt so interested in me? What was my father going to tell me, if he did decide to tell me, about why he hated Dr. Wyatt?

I discovered I was pacing. I looked at my watch; there was ample time to go out and grab a sandwich or some pizza before coming back to do the bedtime rabbit review. But it felt somehow as if it would be too overwhelming to leave the building and come back again. I wasn't tired, exactly, just . . . just . . . And I wasn't hungry, either, although a candy bar wouldn't be a bad thing.

A vision of the extensive vending machine bank in the company cafeteria floated into my mind and before I knew it, I was out in the corridor, locking the lab door carefully behind me.

This part of the building featured floor-to-ceiling glass, and through it I could see the darkness beginning to settle down outside, in the world. The building almost seemed to whisper secrets around me.

I found myself, not heading over to the cafeteria and the vending machines, but instead tracing the route that Foo-foo had taken. And then there I was, in HR, in that dead-end of a corridor, facing the door that hid the little elevator.

This time the door was closed. I read the sign on it. It didn't say "Elevator." It said "Utility Room."

CHAPTER 24

I DIDN'T KNOW exactly why I'd come to look at the hidden elevator. I hadn't really imagined it would be open or that I could examine it closely. Certainly I hadn't thought I'd be able to ride to wherever it went. I assumed it would be locked.

I'd just wanted to see that closed, blank door. Something about the memory of it—drew me.

Utility room.

I stared at the sign and anger filled me. All at once I had to prove to myself that there really was an elevator there; that I hadn't hallucinated it—a modern rabbit hole—as I chased my own white rabbit. I felt my fists clenching and, for one wild moment, I thought that if I just grabbed hold of the handle and wrenched with all my might, I could shear the heavy wooden door right off its hinges. I would reveal the steel sliding elevator door within for all to see. *It would serve them right,* I thought. *Liars!* I pictured Judith Ryan's cobra head.

It was in this mood that I pulled out the card key for my

own laboratory and jammed it into the card reader next to the "utility room." I didn't expect the key to work. I expected it to fail, and that would give me—in my red haze I thought this—a good excuse to wrench the door off.

Okay, I doubt I actually would have tried to break the door. I'd have come to my senses. But I wasn't tested, because—incredibly—the key worked. The card reader clicked smoothly, and its little light flashed green. Disbelieving, I grasped the door and pulled.

It opened easily.

And yes—I had not hallucinated it. There was the elevator inside. It wasn't even closed; its door was fully rolled away into the wall and the interior lay as innocently open and empty and bland as any public elevator in any public building in the land.

As quickly as it had welled up, my anger subsided, leaving a kind of mingled shame and embarrassment behind. I looked down at the card key in my hand. It was a very basic-level security key; programmed, I'd been told, to let me into my own lab and also into public areas like restrooms and lounges. And, apparently, into elevators and utility rooms.

I blew out a long breath. Well. As long as I was here . . .

Feeling foolish but determined, I stepped into the elevator. I looked at the bank of buttons and was hit by a momentary sensation of déjà vu. Then it faded and I understood.

Of course, I'd seen the control panel before, when I'd run in after Foo-foo. I had seen it only for a second, but I realized now that it had stuck in my mind for a reason, and that reason was why I was here right now.

Compared to the other elevators in the building, the control panel had one too many buttons. Ground floor, mezzanine, 1, 2, 3. That was all the same. But beneath that: B1 through B5, where the regular elevators had only B1–B4.

I was sure of this, though I made a mental note to double-check the other elevators before I left tonight.

I reached out gently and pressed the button for B5. It lit up for a second, only to go out as I removed my finger. The elevator door stayed stubbornly open; locked open. I tried three other buttons with the same result. Then I fixed my eyes on a second card key mechanism that sat beside the control panel. Its presence, too, made this elevator different from the others.

Automatically, I tried my card key there, as well. But this time it didn't work. I still couldn't access B5.

Well, what had I expected? This was ridiculous. I was going to leave, right now, and get my head in order.

I got out of the elevator and closed the wooden door firmly. I did not turn again to stare at the utility room sign. Instead, I walked away. Calmly, I checked the inside panel on every single public elevator in the building, where I saw exactly what I expected to see. Four basement levels only.

I went back to my own lab. I spent an hour carefully focused on taking care of the rabbits. At the end of the circuit, I went to stand in front of Foo-foo's cage. I stared at her, and her nose twitched at me.

Okay. Okay, I had somehow managed to creep myself out thoroughly, and I was imagining all sorts of nasty . . . Okay, I was having some attack of senseless paranoia.

Except—at the same time—I didn't believe that I really *was* being paranoid.

Among the great mysteries of biology is the inheritance of what appear to be immutable animal instincts; behaviors that are not necessarily taught by parents to children, but which appear unerringly in the next generation. Spiders spin webs. Birds migrate south to the same places in which their ancestors wintered. Salmon return to spawn in the rivers in which they were originally hatched.

Of course, these behaviors must somehow be genetically coded. After all, if a robin can possess the correct DNA to lay a blue egg, then why shouldn't it possess coding to know just how to build the nest for the egg? It must. It does. Species coding obviously encompasses more than the instructions for an animal's appearance; it encompasses DNA instructions for its behaviors and its instincts.

And since DNA is DNA—the same in a spider as in a human—then why shouldn't humans have instincts that are capable of being just as powerful? Even if we aren't accustomed to thinking of them that way. Even if we generally call them ESP and the subconscious, and more than half distrust what they have to say to us.

These thoughts raced through my head. I wondered, defiantly, if there was any reason why I shouldn't pay attention to the instinct inside of me that was screaming that I knew something, something, something. Why I shouldn't pay attention to the instinct that strung together my mother's long-ago mention of Dr. Wyatt, and my father's hate-filled reaction, and my own doubts about myself, and the silent alert that had gone off inside of me at the sight of that elevator panel. Why I shouldn't pay attention to this . . . and do it as quietly and carefully as my instinct was screaming at me to do.

Why couldn't I trust my own instinct, even if I couldn't understand it?

I went to the computer and set methodically to work. In short order I had discovered that the building plans for Wyatt Transgenics were on file at Cambridge City Hall, in the Inspectional Services Department. Public office hours from 10 to 4, Monday through Friday.

As soon as I could, I was going to check the building plans for that extra subbasement level.

CHAPTER 25

ON SUNDAY—WITH the exception of one short trip to the lab to take care of the rabbits—I stayed home with my father. We planned to sort through my mother's belongings. I was a little shocked when we went into the apartment building's storage area in the morning and I saw the carefully stacked pallet of large plastic containers. I'd known it was there, of course, but I'd always avoided coming in and really looking, really seeing.

The pile of boxes was huge.

My reaction must have been obvious. "I didn't get rid of anything of hers when you and I moved into the building," my father said defensively. "I just packed it all and put it here. It just seemed . . . I couldn't . . ." He shrugged.

"Yeah," I said quickly. "I understand." Of course it wouldn't have been possible for him to give away my mother's things while she lived. It was horribly daunting now, however, to look at the containers. Automatically, I began to count: The pallet was stacked six high, six deep.

By contrast, exactly two small boxes and one suitcase had come from the nursing home. Those had been sufficient to hold her personal belongings for the past few years.

I cleared my throat. "How should we do this? Just start opening things? Make a pile for the donations, another for stuff you want to keep? Maybe I should go get some empty boxes so we can sort things into them."

I looked at my father and saw that he was standing perfectly still beneath the bare overhead lightbulb, with his eyes closed, his arms tight to his sides, and his hands in fists.

"You know," I said, "we don't have to do this today. Next weekend would be fine. This stuff isn't going anywhere on its own."

My father's eyes snapped open and gave me a look that was almost accusing. "I want to do it today."

"Okay. That's fine. Just a thought," I said.

He took a deep breath. "I'm sorry. I need to do it today. I feel I can do it today."

"All right." I eyed the pallet and thought that the only way to do it in a day would be to haul everything off in a truck to the Salvation Army without opening a single container. But even though I knew that my father wanted to donate a lot of the stuff, he had also been clear about planning to sort through everything first. "Let's get started. Why don't I climb up and haul a few containers off the top, and then we can—"

"Eli. Wait."

I turned back to my father.

"I know this is extra work. But I want to bring everything

up to the apartment and sort through it there. If we do it here, anybody can come in anytime."

Now it was my turn to take a deep breath. We lived on the fourth floor! But my father's hands had fisted again and, well, it wasn't my decision anyway. It had to be how *he* wanted it. I felt a surge of protectiveness. If my father wanted privacy, he would have it.

"Okay," I said. "I think I saw a dolly around here someplace that we can borrow to wheel things down the corridor. What if I do the stair part, and you handle the flat stretch with the dolly." I hesitated one last second, thinking of our apartment lined with the containers; piled high with my mother's stuff. It was going to be a disaster area, and in more ways than one. Well, so be it. "Dad, one thing . . ."

"What?"

"We might not get through everything today."

"I know that," said my father. "But I think we might be able to do most of it."

I knew better. It would take many trips just to haul everything upstairs. The irony did not escape me. In my mind I'd been swearing at elevators all night, but now, I'd have done just about anything to be living in a building that had one.

I went to borrow the dolly. Maybe we could at least have everything upstairs by noon, when I'd go off to visit the rabbits.

We did. We managed to fit all the containers into the apartment's living room and hallway, covering the sofa and most of the floor, stacked two and three high. Then, still breathing hard and sweating heavily, I left my father to begin opening the containers alone.

I was gone for an hour and a half. I worked quickly with the rabbits, not only because I was anxious to get home again, but because being inside the Wyatt Transgenics building was now making me feel uneasy. I had barely been able to meet the eyes of the security guard at the front desk when I signed in. I was filled with guilt, although I had done nothing wrong. Nothing but feel determined to chase my instinct about one little elevator. There was nothing bad about that. It was perfectly within the law to examine public building plans.

Yes, whispered a voice in my own head, *perfectly legal—but stupid, too. Why not just go ask Dr. Wyatt directly? Don't you owe him some trust? He's been nothing but good to you. You know what I think? I think you're letting yourself invent something suspicious about Dr. Wyatt because you want to feel closer to your father. But that's dumb, too, because nothing has really changed between you and your father. He still hasn't told you what his problem with Wyatt is. He's still just "thinking about it."*

I shook my head to get rid of the voice. I wasn't going to listen to it today. Today belonged to my father. I could worry about the building plans and the elevator on Monday.

I finished up with the rabbits as quickly as I could and went home, where I found my father sitting cross-legged on the floor. He didn't move or speak, though.

Around him, the room looked as if a tornado had ripped through it. Containers were turned over, upended, their contents—clothing and shoes and books and pictures, a basket of unfinished knitting, a wrapped set of teacups, other strange sundries—were strewn about. And as I gazed around, each object stabbed with its instantaneous familiarity.

That little footstool with the butterfly embroidery on it.

The giant wheel of a Rolodex.

Several dozen red three-ring binders, carefully labeled on their spines.

A beige silk dress.

The skeins of navy wool spilling out of the knitting basket.

Her ancient portable computer that must have weighed twenty pounds.

A single purple Birkenstock sandal.

I said to my father, "Are you okay?"

After a moment, he nodded. He gestured vaguely around the room. "I'm sorry," he said. "I've made a mess. I just . . . I couldn't stop."

"It's all right," I said.

"I can't give it all away," my father said. "We'll pack it all up again, after I've looked at everything, and we'll put it back."

I opened my mouth and then I closed it. "Okay," I said. "Whatever you want."

He looked at me straight on then, and I saw that it *was* actually okay. His eyes were clear and, though sad, totally sane. "I'm sorry," he repeated. "I think I just needed to say that aloud. Of course we won't put everything back in storage. Of course we'll sort through it all and figure out what can go. I'm sure a lot of it . . . some of it . . . can go." He waved one hand vaguely. Then it dropped limply back onto his lap, and I saw that he was holding a photograph album there. It was open.

He looked down at one of the pages and then his shoulders began to shake.

I went and sat down next to him on the floor—shoving aside a pair of high-heeled black pumps to do it—and held him while he cried. "I'm sorry," he said. I shook my head but didn't reply. I tried not to look around. I tried not to see all the stuff.

But then, as he got better control of himself, my father pulled away from me and grabbed the photograph album in his lap. "Look at this," he said to me. "I went looking for this photo and I found it. Look at her. She was eighteen. It was before I ever met her. She was so beautiful. So beautiful."

He pointed. And I could feel his eyes sharply on me as I looked down at the photograph album, into the laughing face of a girl who could have been the sister of Kayla Matheson.

CHAPTER 26

SOMETIMES YOUR EYES play tricks on you. On the street, you catch a glimpse of someone you think you know, but when you get closer, you see you were wrong. The resemblance was an illusion; you can't believe you ever thought it was there.

So I looked away now from the photograph of my mother as a teenager, told myself sternly to be rational, and then looked at the picture again so that the mirage of Kayla, wrongly superimposed on my mother, could fade away.

Except it didn't.

"Eli?" said my father.

I felt as if the floor had dropped away beneath me; as if I had indeed fallen down some rabbit hole into another world where the laws of science had been cross-wired into nonsense. I wondered if I was dreaming. Nightmaring.

"Eli?" said my father again, gently.

I tore my gaze from the photo. His face was all compassion

for me. And was there another expression there—something watchful? "She was the age you are now," he said.

I remembered vomiting behind a bush around the corner from Dr. Wyatt's house. I could see that little boy's face again. *After you puke, you feel better.*

"Eli?"

Genetics enforces one's destiny. One cannot escape.

"She was my age? That's weird to think about. I don't remember seeing this picture before." I tried to make my face and voice ordinary.

"Wasn't she beautiful?" he said again, but I felt sure he was asking me something else. He'd seen Kayla at the memorial service. Or hadn't he? I couldn't remember now. I could ask—except I didn't want to.

I got up. I felt almost feverish; the walls of the room seemed far away and unfocused. "Excuse me," I said. I walked as steadily as possible into the bathroom. I closed the door behind me, marched to the sink, and turned the cold water on full-force. I bent down and splashed my face. Did it again. Again. Again.

Something I had forgotten came back to me. When I was a small child, often when people saw me with my mother, they would remark on our resemblance. *No doubt whose kid that is,* they'd say, smiling.

Nothing odd in a child resembling his mother. Right? But . . . but . . .

I lifted my dripping face and looked into the not-so-clean mirror above the sink. Male and female features seemed to transmute, to melt into each other. My mother—Kayla—me. I lifted my fist to smash the mirror and barely caught myself in time, knuckles half an inch from its surface.

I pulled in a breath. Let it out. Another.

"Eli?" My father was outside the bathroom door. "You've been in there awhile. Is everything okay?"

Another breath. I lowered my fist from the mirror and with both hands, gripped the sink. Then: "Yes," I called above the noise of the running water. "Fine. I'll be in here a few more minutes, though. Okay?" The sink was full now. I turned off the water.

"Okay." I heard his footsteps as he moved away.

What the hell did it mean?

I lowered my head back to the sink. Cold water.

Thought, analysis, were still impossible. I decided not to try, just yet.

Cold water.

Eventually, I toweled my face and head dry. Then, without making any conscious decision, I groped for my cell phone. With some difficulty, I made my fingers work well enough to call Viv at home. The line rang once. Twice. Then Viv picked up, and at the sound of her voice, I felt the ground beneath me steady.

I didn't say hello or my name or anything polite. I didn't have the ability to say anything but what was most important. "Viv. Can I come see you now?"

There was a moment of complete silence. Then: "Yes." Viv said it as if we were still together, as if it were perfectly ordinary for me to call. Another moment of silence in which I simply breathed, groping for the words that I knew must be necessary, but not finding any. Then Viv added calmly, "Mom's at Bill's. I'm alone here," and I knew that she was allowing me not to have to say anything else. Not to have to explain.

Or beg.

"I'll be there in ten minutes," I said. I hung up. I clutched the sink for a moment longer and just breathed. Then I left the apartment like a heat-seeking missile, taking only the time to call over my shoulder, "Gotta go feed the rabbits again."

And when I got to Viv's and she let me in, and she took one look at my face and then simply opened her arms, at that moment I understood what she'd been trying to say all along about trust. I saw that underneath everything, she had had it for me. And that—at that moment—finally, shakily, so did I, for her.

"I had no right to come here like this," I said to her, later. We had been silent together a long time. "I want you to know that I know that."

"Shh." Viv's eyes were so clear. "You do have the right, Eli. I give it to you."

We were in her bed in her room. We were mostly naked. I curled my body entirely around hers and held her. I felt her move her head so that her cheek brushed my arm. I could still feel the fear in me, and the bewilderment, but it was at a distance. I was safe, for now. And, slowly, an idea came to me.

"Could you do something for me tomorrow morning?" I asked Viv.

"If it's before noon. After that I have to go to work."

"Could you go to city hall and look up some building plans?"

"That's it? All right. For what building? And what do you want me to look for?"

"The building's Wyatt Transgenics." I hesitated, because part of me knew that if I did this myself, it would be easier and cleaner. Would Viv be able to read a blueprint for a building she'd never been in? But Viv had turned in my arms and was looking at me with interest and—yes—pleasure at being asked. She could tell I was about to open up. It was what she'd wanted all along, and it was something I could give her now. A little bit, anyway.

"I need you to count the number of subterranean levels in the building plan," I said. "Look through every page of the plan. It might be that one section of the building has more basement levels than another section. I just want to know what the plans actually call for."

"Okay," Viv said. She was regarding me thoughtfully. "I can do that."

"You're wondering why I want to know," I said.

She nodded. "Yes, but—"

"Well, it's that—"

"Wait," Viv cut in. She had a very determined look on her face. "It's okay, Eli. You don't have to tell me. I can just go and get the information for you. I don't need to know why. You'll tell me when you're ready. Or not."

"But—"

"I was thinking about what you said. Before, you know." She ducked her head, then raised it to look at me straight on. "I've realized that I was wrong and you were right. About respecting privacy, I mean. I don't expect you to tell me everything you think and feel."

"Oh," I said. I took her hand. "And here I'd just about decided you were right and I was wrong."

She frowned. "Really?"

"Well," I said. "There might always be things I need to keep to myself. But I want you to understand that it won't be because I don't trust you. And—and love you. I do—I love you, Vivian Fadiman. And I trust you."

Viv's hand turned in mine. She gripped it hard. Then she smiled. "I know," she said. "I know that now."

CHAPTER 27

THE NEXT MORNING, early, while my father's exhausted snores resonated through the apartment, I returned home to the apartment, stepping over and around the piles of things in the living room until I'd made my way to the photograph album. I located the picture of my mother, the picture that so closely resembled Kayla Matheson. I looked at it for an entire minute, just to be sure I hadn't imagined their resemblance.

I hadn't, though on close examination Kayla and my mother were not as similar as I had at first thought. It wasn't just that Kayla was more beautiful, more perfect. Her eyes were a little different—narrower. And their noses were quite dissimilar. For a second I was filled with relief. But then my unease returned. There was still something here that was worrisome. These were two girls that you'd instantly know—*know!*—were closely related. I did not believe it was a coincidence. I could not.

And whatever this resemblance was, whatever it meant, I

was involved in it somehow. Finding out about it would not just mean finding out some things about Kayla and/or my mother that I didn't really want to know. It would mean finding out some truth about me. Some secret knowledge waited within me like a shark lurks in the darkest, uncharted depths of the sea, and it had been with me, on some level, always. Always.

I acknowledged it now. I said it aloud, softly. "Something is strange about you, Eli Samuels. Something is very strange." And as I heard the words, I could feel their truth.

Something was strange within me. Yes. But . . .

But it wasn't Huntington's disease.

My mother had had HD, but I didn't. I suddenly knew that, knew it with a sureness and ferocity that needed no confirming genetic tests. I *knew* it—and I knew why I knew it.

I put a hand against the wall to support myself as memory rose in me.

I am seven.

We are seated at the kitchen table; my mother, my father, and me. The silence around us is thick as smoke, and I sense that I should be quiet. My parents are each looking at sections of the newspaper, and I have a book in front of me, but none of us are reading. We are waiting, though I don't know what for.

Then the phone rings.

My father leaps frantically to answer it, nearly overturning his chair, and my mother grabs me from my own chair and up in her arms. My book falls open onto the floor. We ignore it. She holds me tightly. We watch my father on the telephone.

"Mrs. Emerson. I've been waiting for your call." He is quiet, listening intently. "You're sure?" he says. "You're absolutely sure?"

A moment later, his face is alight with joy. Transcendence. He whirls and yells to my mother, "It's no! Ava, it's no! They'll send a letter as well . . ."

He says a few more words into the phone, but I don't hear them. I feel my mother bury her face in my hair. I feel her heart pounding hard against my cheek.

Then my father hangs up the phone and comes over. He puts his arms around us both. "Eli is okay," he says. "Ava, our little boy tested negative. Thank God."

My mother exhales, hard. She says, "I told you. I told you to believe in him."

My father is silent a moment. Then he says, "Yes. You did tell me. You did tell me he was honorable. I guess you were right. About this, anyway. Thank God."

"Stop thanking God." There is an edge to her voice. "He got us into this mess. Thank Dr. Wyatt."

There is a long moment of silence. For some reason I feel that I can't, shouldn't, move, or the world will shatter around us.

Then my father says, "I suppose."

"We couldn't have done it without him," my mother insists. "It was the only way. And now Eli is negative. No matter what happens to me—our son will be fine. That's all that matters."

"I love you, Ava," my father says.

"I know," whispers my mother. But I can tell she is not looking at him. Her head is still turned down, and her lips are still pressed against the top of my head. "I know. I thank you for letting me do what I had to do. Maybe now you can let go of the rest."

My father does not reply directly. He simply says, again, "I love you." And then he adds, "And I love our son. No matter what, that wasn't a mistake. Since the moment we knew you were pregnant—Ava, I've always known that couldn't be wrong . . . no matter how it came about."

"I know," whispers my mother again.

Still holding the photograph of my mother, I got up from the floor. I went over to the hall table, where I'd replaced the HD-negative letter, burying it under the mound of old mail that filled the drawer. I had a clear photographic memory of the letter—it had seared itself into my brain on the day I'd read it—but I wanted to look at it again. I needed to be completely sure that I had not made all of this up.

It took me a few minutes to find the letter, but I did, and I opened it. My eyes went directly to its signature.

Harriet Emerson, MSW. Genetic Counselor.

Mrs. Emerson. I've been waiting for your call.

Next, the date: *July, 1993.* When I was seven. When testing for Huntington's first became available to anyone who wanted it—any adult, that is.

Finally, the key sentence: *As per Dr. Wyatt's request and referral, we have tested your blood sample and can confirm that you are negative for Huntington's disease.*

It had not been my father's blood sample that had been sent in—by Dr. Wyatt—for testing. It had been mine. I had been tested as soon as the procedure was available, even though it was not legal to test a child. I had been tested, I supposed, because my parents had needed to know, for sure.

And Dr. Wyatt had helped them. He had sent my blood sample in, claiming that it was from my father.

CHAPTER 28

THE CONNECTION BETWEEN my parents, Dr. Wyatt, and me was now clear. Well . . . clearer. Something illegal had been done. I should not have been tested as a child.

But that didn't strike me as being such a big deal. I could easily understand why my parents had done it. The early, secretive, illegal test didn't begin to explain my father's hostility toward Dr. Wyatt, though. Wouldn't he have simply been grateful for Dr. Wyatt's assistance?

I looked at the photograph of my mother, which I had placed on the hall table. Kayla's resemblance to my mother was not explained, either. For a second I thought of my very first theory: that my mother had had an affair with Dr. Wyatt. I was surprised at the rush of hope this thought now gave me. It was so . . . so ordinary.

But I didn't believe it. I couldn't believe it. And the reason I couldn't was because of the other thing that was not explained. My niggling knowledge, my bone-deep awareness that—even though it wasn't HD—there was still something very peculiar about me. Something very peculiar that had always been there.

Turns out Swampy isn't a man who's turned into a plant. Swampy's a plant that tried to become a man.

Of course I didn't think I was a plant. But—for the first time I allowed a question about my origins to arise fully in my conscious mind from where it had lurked inside me . . . well, forever.

Since the moment we knew you were pregnant—Ava, I've always known that couldn't be wrong . . . no matter how it came about.

What had my father meant by "no matter how it came about"? How had I come to be?

Kayla's resemblance to my mother—was Kayla my sister? Half sister?

I fished in the drawer for the box of envelopes, slipped the photo of my mother into one, and put the envelope into my backpack. Determination filled me. I would get answers, and I would not allow my mind to run wild before I did.

Facts. I needed facts.

I would go to Wyatt Transgenics today, and I would find Dr. Wyatt there, and I would show him the photograph. I wouldn't tell him about the HD test—that was between me and my father. But I would demand—well, I would ask for— an explanation about Kayla.

A particularly loud snore came from my father's room, and my eyes went automatically to the hallway. A second later, I found I had picked my way back through the piles of my mother's things and moved to stand outside his bedroom door.

Going through my mother's belongings yesterday had seemed to do my father some good. In fact, when I'd come back home this morning, after the time with Viv, I found that he had actually packed some things away in a box, labeled firmly for charity. It was a start. And he'd slept. The snores were evidence.

He would get better, my father. He had decades ahead of him. I leaned my forehead against the door of his bedroom, listening to the snores as they came strongly, regularly. My father could have a good life now, without my mother. He could heal in the days and weeks and years ahead.

He had promised me that he would think about telling me what had happened between him and Dr. Wyatt. As far as I knew, he was still thinking . . . and I would go on letting him. I would give him all the time he needed. I would not go to him with my new memory, or with the letter. I would take my questions to Dr. Wyatt instead.

And—despite all the things I'd told myself, and Viv, last night, about trust—I wasn't ready to talk to Viv yet, either. I couldn't be sure what Viv would think if she knew I was uneasy about more than the number of basement levels at Wyatt Transgenics. If she knew about Kayla. If she knew about . . . well, about Swampy.

I stepped away from my father's bedroom door. "Sleep well, Dad," I whispered.

At work, I showed my badge at the front desk and loped up the double-helix staircase two steps at a time. At the top, I turned left instead of right, and marched like a tin soldier to Dr. Wyatt's cramped office, the same one in which he'd interviewed me only a few weeks ago.

The door was open.

Dr. Wyatt was inside, sitting in the same dangerously one-armed chair that I remembered from before. He was writing rapidly on a yellow legal pad. After a couple of minutes, understanding that he wasn't going to look up on his own, I rapped on the open door. Once. Twice. Then a third time, much harder. "Dr. Wyatt?" I almost bellowed his name.

Dr. Wyatt's head jerked. I had the feeling I'd awoken someone from a deep sleep. But then he turned to face the doorway and saw me. "Eli!" he said, and smiled. He looked so absolutely delighted to see me. I couldn't help it—I smiled back.

"Hello," I said.

He waved me inside his office. I closed the door behind me. I didn't want interruptions.

Dr. Wyatt didn't appear to notice or care about the door. He was looking at my face, examining it just as thoroughly as he had on the first day we'd met. I waited, as I had then. And eventually he said, "I heard about your mother's death, of course. Are you okay?"

The kindness on his face—the honesty and rightness of his not saying the pointless *I'm sorry*—overset me for a second. I managed to nod. What had I been thinking? I had turned him into some kind of monster in my mind, but he was no such thing.

"I'm okay," I said.

After another moment of examining my face, he shook his head. "No. Something is bothering you. What is it?"

I drew in a breath, and then let it out. "It's just—I have a question for you. It's about my mother."

"Yes?" Dr. Wyatt said.

I reached into my backpack and pulled out the picture. My hand was shaking as I gave it to him. "This is my mother," I said. "When she was a teenager."

Dr. Wyatt took the photo. He examined it for a bare second before looking up again at me. "Yes?"

"She looks like Kayla Matheson," I burst out. "She could be her sister!"

Dr. Wyatt nodded. "Yes," he said simply.

For a moment I thought that would be all. For a moment I thought Dr. Wyatt would claim it was a coincidence and send me away.

But he didn't. He continued, smoothly: "Good for you, Eli. Good for you for coming to talk to me about it. I was hoping you would, sometime. In fact, I was surprised and disappointed that you didn't recognize Kayla at once, when you met her. I got her here to Cambridge for the summer on purpose to meet you."

I stared at him.

"But of course, you didn't know your mother when she was young," he said. "The resemblance is remarkable. Those genes bred true."

CHAPTER 29

THERE WASN'T AN EXTRA CHAIR in the room. I leaned up against the second table, opposite Dr. Wyatt. I realized I'd dropped my backpack onto the floor by my feet.

"I'm sorry, Eli." Dr. Wyatt was frowning. "I see from your face that this truly is a surprise. I'm afraid I assumed you knew about my association with your mother—that that was why you contacted me in the first place—but that you just weren't ready to talk to me about it yet."

"No," I said steadily. "I told you what I knew when I came in here that first time. My mother used to mention you. My father disliked hearing your name. I knew who you were from looking you up, and from science classes at school, and from reading newspapers. I was curious. Maybe I had an instinct that there was more—I think I must have. But nothing concrete."

Except that . . . when I wrote that initial email to Dr. Wyatt, I had actually been in pursuit of what I was now on the brink of learning. I was getting what I'd asked for, even if until now I hadn't fully let myself know I was asking for it. Somewhere in me, I had known . . . something.

"I see," said Dr. Wyatt. He was still holding the photograph of my mother. He looked down at it and then up at me. "I'm not sure what I should tell you—what you want to know. How much, that is. If you're ready . . . ?"

I swallowed. "Okay. Just tell me this: Is Kayla related to my mother? To me? And what about my dad?" I backed up around the table I'd been leaning against and sank down to sit on the carpet, facing Dr. Wyatt. I pressed my back against the wall. I tightened my arms around my knees.

Dr. Wyatt put down the photo. His voice brightened. "Well! The problem is that the word 'related' is old-fashioned and inexact. The right way for you to look at it is to understand that you and Kayla have some DNA in common."

I understood all of the words he'd just said, but I didn't know what they meant together. "Do you mean my mother is Kayla's mother? That Kayla is my half sister? Or . . . or . . ." I stopped.

Dr. Wyatt said, quietly, compassionately: "Yes. Or."

I exhaled. I had a sudden vision of Foo-foo. She and her transgenic sister rabbits were valuable because they produced a kind of milk that their "normal" sisters did not. For each transgenic rabbit now up in the lab, there had first been a normal rabbit egg, and a normal rabbit sperm. Creation: a fertilized egg. But then . . . careful insertion of the right DNA to bend the development path . . .

I said abruptly, "My mother had Huntington's disease. And

I don't. I know I don't; I saw the letter with the test results. What I don't know is why. Because it's not just that I got lucky in the genetic lottery, is it? My father said something . . . I never was at risk—right?"

"No," said Dr. Wyatt steadily. "You were not at risk, ever. I made sure of that—with your mother."

We looked at each other straight on. "Tell me," I said. "Tell me how."

Dr. Wyatt's cheeks had taken on a rosy cast. "Well, I have to confess that I'm still proud of myself, because this was nearly two decades ago. But—oh, I'll be as concise as possible, and we can discuss the science of it later on, eh?"

I managed to nod.

"You don't have Huntington's because your mother came to me for help. We'd met casually at Harvard, where I was doing a series of guest lectures one semester. This was before actual HD testing was available, but Ava told me that she knew she was at risk. And that she wanted a child anyway—a healthy child."

I hardly dared to breathe.

"We'd known the location of the genetic marker for HD since 1983," Dr. Wyatt went on. "But even though there was as yet no way to test Ava directly, and wouldn't be for years, she asked if I might be able to spot the HD marker on an egg." He leaned forward intently. "I didn't realize at the time that it was a question that would change the course of my intellectual life. But I did know I was intrigued. It was all highly, er, irregular, but I wanted to try. I couldn't resist trying!

"So. The idea was that Ava would undergo hormone therapy to produce a clutch of eggs. I would harvest them from her—very standard fertility treatment—and then see if I could isolate some viable eggs that definitely did not have HD. Then, with your father's cooperation, we could fertilize and implant those healthy embryos in your mother's uterus and hope at least one developed normally."

"Me." The word escaped from me.

"You," Dr. Wyatt confirmed. He smiled. "Simple," he said. "And—if I do say so myself—elegant."

CHAPTER 30

I COULD FEEL THAT MY MOUTH had dropped open. Despite the fact that this story involved me personally, my brain stirred with pure intellectual interest. It did sound simple. But then— especially if this had been possible and perfectible twenty years ago—why didn't everybody do it? "Was this legal?" I asked.

A look of impatience crossed Dr. Wyatt's face. "What a stupid thing to focus on, Eli. I thought you'd be interested in the *science* here—once you got past wallowing in the personal revelations, of course.

"I have no idea if we violated some minor law—nor do I care. This was twenty years ago. If you're asking about medical competence, I have an MD as well as a PhD. While certainly I wasn't operating a licensed fertility clinic, I knew precisely what I was attempting to do, my technique was impeccable, and there was no danger to Ava. I also knew—as did Ava— that no ordinary clinic could have helped her. None of them had my specialized knowledge or expertise. Or—may I add—daring."

"Oh," I said uncertainly.

Dr. Wyatt wasn't through. His stare bored into me. "Moreover, it was a private matter. How a couple chooses to go about having a baby—or indeed, in the future, chooses the genetic makeup of that baby—should be entirely their own business and their own choice. Not the government's. Don't you agree with that? Eli?"

It did sound sensible and correct. "Yes. I'm sorry. I wasn't thinking. All of this is a lot to absorb."

"Well, take your time." Dr. Wyatt leaned toward me, his right wrist resting heedlessly on the broken arm of the chair. "Anything else you want to know? Ask me the important questions, the scientific questions. Come on."

One thing was pressing at me urgently, though I doubted that it was the kind of question Dr. Wyatt meant when he said "important" and "scientific." It probably fit under "wallowing in personal revelations." Dr. Wyatt had mentioned my father's "cooperation." But my father was angry at Dr. Wyatt . . .

I understood the basic workings of in vitro fertilization; we used it with the rabbits. The unfertilized eggs were removed from the female, and were then fertilized in the lab using donor sperm—

"Eli?" Dr. Wyatt prompted. "I know you have good questions."

I did—but they weren't scientific. What would my father say when I went home and told him what I'd learned? Why did my father hate Dr. Wyatt so much, if Dr. Wyatt had helped him and my mother have me, their much-desired HD-negative child? Would my father finally tell me everything he knew once he learned how much I had put together myself?

Did I now want him to?

"Eli." Impatience now. "Come on."

"Kayla," I said aloud. "You said Kayla and I have some shared DNA—my mother's DNA, right?"

Dr. Wyatt nodded. "Yes."

"How did that happen?"

Dr. Wyatt was smiling again. "You tell *me* about Kayla. You have the ability to figure it out." He was acting as if this were some kind of test he knew I could pass, and once more I found I wanted to prove myself to him, to please him.

But I wasn't sure I could figure this out.

"I don't understand about Kayla," I said slowly. "Because she's a little older than I am. If she—if the egg that became Kayla was . . . was viable, why go on to have me?" And as I uttered that question, others crowded up in my brain after it: Why did Kayla have different parents, the Mathesons? Was Mrs. Matheson a surrogate mother, or an adoptive mother? Who was Kayla's genetic father—or was that somehow not relevant? Dr. Wyatt had said Kayla and I shared genetic material; he hadn't said we were siblings.

"It took a while to get everything working properly," Dr. Wyatt was explaining. "Several cycles of eggs, as I recall, before I succeeded with you. Kayla's egg was from an earlier cycle."

It wasn't an answer to my question. Or was it? I tried to remember all I knew, from the rabbits, about in vitro fertilization.

"Not all eggs can be successfully fertilized," I said. "And not all fertilized eggs grow successfully, either in the lab or later, after they've been implanted."

Dr. Wyatt was smiling encouragingly again, like the mentor I'd hoped he would be. "And why is that?"

"Sometimes cells don't divide properly, or at all. So, you can produce a number of eggs in an in vitro cycle, but you have no guarantee any of them will become babies—um, that is, viable embryos."

"That's right," said Dr. Wyatt approvingly. "There are usually waste products along the way."

I winced, hearing that, though upstairs in Larry's lab, and in the textbooks I'd read, I'd just taken the term for granted. But we were talking about my mother's eggs, my potential sisters and brothers.

Waste products.

"But Kayla . . . that is, the fertilized egg that became Kayla—obviously that must have been viable," I said. "She exists. So how come she—" It sounded ridiculous, but I said it anyway. "How come she isn't me? Isn't leading my life, I mean? How come I exist at all?"

The more I thought about it, the stranger it all seemed. I stared at Dr. Wyatt. "You didn't really answer me before. You said Kayla wasn't my sister, that we had some shared DNA. But she did come from one of my mother's eggs, right?"

"Right," said Dr. Wyatt.

"Then I don't understand," I said flatly. "Is she my sister, or half sister—or isn't she?"

Dr Wyatt sighed, but his eyes were almost twinkling with

excitement as he watched me. "Think like a scientist, Eli. A geneticist. What are the possibilities here? Try listing them in your mind."

I tried. Gene transfers . . . surrogate mothers . . . gene defects that weren't fatal . . . fertilization . . .

And then I felt myself go cold and still, deep inside, as I realized that this line of reasoning took me inexorably back to the question of my father. Maybe it wouldn't have taken a scientist there, but I wasn't a scientist—at least, not yet. I *could* think of a reason why the egg that became Kayla might not have been acceptable: if the sperm donor were not my father. And that possibility took me to questions concerning my mother and this alliance of hers with Dr. Wyatt . . . The questions spiraled away from me in an endless helix that resembled not at all the structured, ordered beauty of DNA.

I thought: *I have to talk to my dad.* I cannot continue this conversation until I have talked to him. I have betrayed him by coming to Dr. Wyatt first. He deserves better from me. I have betrayed him.

And like a miracle, at that moment, my cell phone rang. It trilled out shrilly from my backpack. "Mine," I said foolishly to Dr. Wyatt. I scrabbled for it.

"Let it take a message," said Dr. Wyatt, but I ignored him and looked at the face of the phone, where the caller was identified: It was Viv. "It's my dad," I lied. "I have to take it. Sorry. I'll talk to you later."

"But this is important—"

"Sorry!" I said. I bolted for the door of the office, grabbing the handle, practically racing to get out. And once I was outside, once I was halfway down the corridor, once I was away, away, I pressed the button on the phone that would connect me to Viv. Hearing her voice in my ear was so wonderful that at first I couldn't focus on what exactly she was saying. "Could you repeat that?" I asked.

"I'm just outside city hall," Viv said patiently. "I found the architect's plans, no problem. I even got copies for you to look at later."

I had forgotten that I'd sent Viv to look at the building plans for Wyatt Transgenics. I exhaled. It seemed so minor now, that I'd been curious about a discrepancy in buttons on elevators. But Viv did have the information. "How many basement levels do the plans specify?" I asked.

"Four."

My stride had taken me some distance. I was on the mezzanine. I lowered my voice. "Throughout the entire building? Not four in the east wing and, say, five in the west? You're sure?"

"I'm sure," said Viv. "Only four."

CHAPTER 31

I LEFT WYATT TRANSGENICS bare minutes later via the front door. As I walked away from the building, I called the lab on my cell phone and recorded a message for Mary Alice. I knew she would be okay with my not coming in; both she and Larry had told me to take all the time off I needed.

As I walked home, I thought obsessively about Kayla. How much did she know about her own origins? Did she know that she and I had—Dr. Wyatt's phrase—*shared DNA*? I couldn't wrap my mind around that, though. To me it seemed clear that our relationship was simpler: We had the same biological mother.

Right? Wrong?

Think like a geneticist, Dr. Wyatt had said.

Larry, on my very first day at work: *You know what "transgenic" means? It's when an organism is altered by having a gene from another species transferred into it.*

Okay. If you could recombine genes from different species,

just as we did with the rabbits, you could, obviously, recombine genes within a single species. The technology for exchanging DNA inside a zygote was wildly inexact, generally requiring multiple tries to get it right—and mostly, it never went right anyway. But it could be done, theoretically. There was even a scientific term for a being that was created by the experimental recombination of DNA from different sources. That term was *chimera*.

And if anyone would have been capable of creating a human chimera twenty years ago—if anyone would have been capable of creating a viable human embryo from a fertilized egg in which DNA from multiple human sources was recombined—it would have been Dr. Wyatt.

Was that what Dr. Wyatt had meant? That Kayla was not my sister, or my half sister—and was not the child my parents had ordered—because she was a human chimera? Had she been pieced together by recombining DNA from several donor sources, only one of whom—albeit the all-important original egg—was my mother? Was Kayla like a creature from science fiction: a bunch of sewn-together genes from a host of parent-donors? A more sophisticated, high-tech Frankenstein's monster—beautiful, smart, athletic, perfect—because she had been deliberately designed to be that way? Because Dr. Wyatt was brilliant enough to succeed where anyone else would have failed?

And if so—what about me?

But no, I knew who my father was! He'd *cooperated;* Dr. Wyatt had said so. I was simply the HD-negative child my mother had wanted. There had been no genetic alterations to my DNA . . . just a careful selecting of an egg with a normal chromosome four.

I felt my pace speed up. I tried to tell myself that Dr. Wyatt was lying. Had to be lying. Even today, let alone twenty years ago, most attempts to create animal chimeras were unsuccessful. One in two or three hundred would be a miraculous success rate. Humans were so complex—and, even with hormones and the several cycles Dr. Wyatt had mentioned, my mother couldn't have produced very many eggs. Not hundreds. A couple dozen, at best? I wasn't sure.

But Kayla did exist. And she looked like my mother . . .

Think like a geneticist.

Well, that didn't just mean thinking about scientific possibilities. It also meant considering the scientific realities. There was a lot of reason not to believe Dr. Wyatt. Even today, despite the existence of the human genome map, it would be almost *impossible* to do detailed genetic manipulation on an embryo and come up with something so . . . so perfect as Kayla. It wasn't as if one gene usually mapped neatly to one trait. The impact of specific genes on development, the importance of environmental factors—it was all still largely unclear. So, if you were trying to create a human chimera, how could you possibly know what genes to swap in? How would you know what genes would make for beauty? For intelligence?

The answer was that you could not know. You'd be working blindly. You'd be at the mercy of chance. Dr. Wyatt was a genius, sure, but even he could not have done it. Not today—and certainly not twenty years ago.

Here was a much more scientifically plausible idea: Kayla was the product of my mother's egg, some guy's sperm—Dr. Wyatt himself?—and a surrogate mother. Her father wouldn't have been my father, obviously, or Kayla would have been the child my parents raised rather than me. Maybe she'd been a "dry run" before me—to see if Dr. Wyatt could successfully check chromosome four.

I winced, though, and I wasn't quite sure why. If any of this was true, Dr. Wyatt really had accomplished something amazing—something with great potential for helping alleviate human suffering, as he had said. Why was I feeling so horrified at both the "dry run" and the chimera theories? Was it just personal wallowing?

My mind flitted off to the realm of the law. Suppose, just for a second, that making a human chimera was possible. It had to be illegal. You couldn't do medical experiments with human embryos. The government wouldn't allow it. Would they?

But then I remembered that it had taken years after research began before the U.S. government began even talking about the possible ethics and legality of using embryonic human tissues in that research. Why would there, then, have been a law against the making of human chimeras twenty years ago? It was unlikely.

I could turn around and sprint back to Wyatt Transgenics right now. I could go up to Dr. Wyatt's office and say to him, "Chimera." And if that were the scientific answer he'd been looking for, he'd tell me so. *Excellent work!* he would say. Then he'd add, *Any other questions?*

He would be pleased with me.

But I kept walking toward home and my father. If I was going to learn anything else, I needed it to be from him.

When I reached home, I pounded up the stairs to the apartment, unlocked the door, and was warmed by the obvious gladness on my father's face when he saw me.

"Hello!" He was seated on the floor of the chaotic living room, sorting books into various boxes. "This is a nice surprise. I thought you'd be at work all day—is everything all right?"

"Yeah," I said. Then I was tongue-tied. I looked into his clear, calm eyes and knew that he had found his way to some peace, at least at this moment . . . and I didn't want to mess with that. Didn't want to say *clutch of eggs* and *let's talk about the girl who looks like Mom* and *I have to insist that you discuss Dr. Wyatt with me now*. Not yet. Not at this second. Maybe later today. Maybe tomorrow. There was no rush, after all.

"I decided to take the rest of the day off," I said. "I thought you could use help with the packing."

"I could," said my father. "I'm feeling ambitious to get it all done as quickly as we can."

"Let's do it," I said.

We sorted and packed all afternoon. At five o'clock, with my father's permission (and a lack of questions, for which I was grateful—though he was hiding a grin), I called Viv and invited her to join us. Then the three of us hung out together in the living room throughout the evening, still working, with Bach playing quietly on the CD player and a couple of pizzas ordered for dinner.

It felt ordinary. It felt wonderful. Viv and my father and I talked with surprising ease and enjoyment about regular things—the superiority of bananas to every other kind of fruit, whether instant messaging and email were going to destroy formal English spelling, how it was that special effects had ruined the later *Star Wars* movies but made *The Matrix,* why you never got tired of eating pizza.

I found myself thinking, *This is the life that I want.* And during those few hours with the two people I cared about most, I let myself believe that I could have it. That the things I'd learned that day from Dr. Wyatt—the things I knew I still had to learn—would make no difference.

The illusion was strengthened by the way the evening ended, with my father standing up and stretching, saying he was off to bed, and mouthing to me, over Viv's head, "It's okay to invite her to stay."

So I did.

We didn't have sex; I was too self-conscious with my father nearby, and I think Viv was, too. But I held her while she slept, and then I slept, too, for a while.

CHAPTER 32

I WOKE UP SUDDENLY and fully in the pitch dark. Viv moved, and I said, softly: "You awake?"

"Yes. What time is it?"

I reached for the clock and pressed the little button that made its numbers glow in the dark. "Two thirty-eight."

"Oh." Then: "I was only pretending to sleep before. I'm not—I don't think I really can. I don't seem to be tired."

"Me either," I said.

We were quiet a while longer, and then Viv said, "I'm wondering, Eli—could you tell me why you asked me to look up the building plans for Wyatt Transgenics? What's with the subbasement? I've been eaten up with curiosity about it all day."

"Oh," I said. "Right. That." I reached over to the nightstand and turned on the lamp.

With everything else that had happened that day, I'd mostly forgotten about the discrepancy in basement levels at Wyatt Transgenics. I couldn't even remember why the issue had ever seemed important enough to investigate—especially after I'd learned that my own card key worked to open the little mislabeled elevator. I now thought that I'd simply projected my real anxieties about Dr. Wyatt and my own past onto the red herring issue of the basement.

Viv was leaning forward, though, waiting, and so I told her the story of how I'd chased Foo-foo around the building and into the hidden elevator, of the look on Judith Ryan's face when I'd practically trampled her, and of my discovery of the different numbers on the elevator's control panel. "I'm not sure why I wanted to know what the city hall blueprints showed," I finished—and only then realized that I'd gotten out of bed and had been pacing as I talked. "There's probably some simple reason for the discrepancy. But it just seemed—I don't know . . ."

"Strange." Viv had shifted so that she was lying on her stomach, her chin propped up in her hands. "And yeah, probably there's some innocent explanation, but it's not an *obvious* explanation. I personally find it very odd that there's a basement level that isn't on the official record, and that's accessed through an elevator labeled 'Utility Room.' I mean, why?"

"Yeah." I flung myself down on the bed again next to Viv. She smiled right into my eyes, and I found myself grinning back.

And all at once, it was one of those magical moments between us. "I'm thinking retroviruses," she said. "Horrible new diseases developed in secret by a dastardly cadre of mad scientists. Of course, we're the only ones who suspect anything—and if we don't act, the world will surely be destroyed."

"No, no," I said. "It's a race of genius rabbits. This is only one of many thousands of basement warrens that they've carved out beneath the laboratories of the United States. They're pursuing their own scientific agenda. They hypnotized Judith Ryan, and she assists them by—by—"

"—by delivering Gap toddler-sized T-shirts and shorts to the basement for the rabbits. They only wear one hundred percent cotton, naturally. And as for Foo-foo—"

"Foo-foo is obviously on an undercover spy mission. She hypnotized me to let her out of her cage and was making her way back to Mission Control when I thwarted her—"

"Stupid, hulking human! Don't you realize that you risk the wrath of the entire Rabbit Empire?"

"I'm scared," I said. I reached over and put my hand on top of hers. She turned her hand and interlinked her fingers with mine.

"Yes," she said to me, and her voice was suddenly entirely serious. "You are."

I just looked at her. She swallowed and continued. All the fun had drained from her voice, her face. "Something's different about you. Something important." I saw her entire body tighten, and then she blurted: "Did you take the blood test for HD?"

That startled me. I shook my head, because I hadn't taken it for myself, after all, and that was what Viv meant. "No. But I've decided that I will take the test," I said, realizing only as the words came out that they were true.

Viv nodded gravely. "Would you like me to go with you?"

"I need to bring my father," I said, again discovering my intention as I spoke. "But thank you."

She smiled at me. We were quiet a while longer, but the silence remained charged with something I couldn't interpret. Suddenly Viv twisted her hand out of mine. Her face was still only inches from mine, though, and never had I seen her look more serious.

"There's one more thing, then," she said. "And it's trivial next to HD, and—and I don't really care; I decided it doesn't matter, we were broken up, and now we're back together and that's what matters. But . . ."

"But what?" I said.

Viv bit her lip.

I put my arms around her. "Viv—"

"I'm sorry," she burst out. "I have to know. It'll be okay, but I have to know. You were with some other girl while you weren't with me. Right?"

I was appalled. And I felt guilty, even though—luckily—she was wrong. I said cautiously, "No, Viv. I wasn't. Why would you think that?"

"Because." She swallowed hard, and then continued remorselessly. "There was this girl at your mother's memorial service. She had very long brown hair and was wearing a pale pink flowered dress. She came in late. She was totally gorgeous, even if she didn't have a clue that you shouldn't wear a pink halter dress to a funeral.

"She sat and watched you the whole time the service was going on. I saw you turn and see her. You smiled at her. Don't even think of trying to tell me you don't remember, because you'd remember her even if you didn't know her. Anyone would—including me! But you did know her. And then I saw her walking over to talk to you afterward. That was when I left."

"Oh," I said. I let Viv go. I didn't mean to, but somehow my arms loosened and she shifted away from me. I said, "I didn't realize you'd seen her."

"Well, I did."

"I didn't date her," I said. "Or—or anything. Really." The thought that I'd found Kayla desirable now made me feel queasy. And had I imagined, because Kayla was so beautiful and because I'd wanted her, that Dr. Wyatt had thrown us together deliberately, hoping we'd be interested in each other romantically? I found myself thinking of the Egyptian pharaohs—they'd married and had children with their sisters. But it was genetically unsound to interbreed; everyone knew that. Except—well, with plants and animals, if you were doing deliberate work to develop a species, you did interbreed. That was how you encouraged certain traits to emerge. And Dr. Wyatt was a geneticist . . . *Think like a scientist* . . .

A whisper emerged from Viv. "Eli, look. There was something about her. There was something about the two of you, together. It's not that I don't believe you, but—well, you have to talk to me." She had her arms around her knees and was looking directly at me. She was squinting . . . or maybe guarding against tears. But nonetheless her voice was firm. And I looked at Viv as she sat in my bed and I knew that I would do whatever I had to do to make sure it wasn't the last time she was there. Even if it meant being completely open with her.

I said, "Her name is Kayla Matheson. And . . ." I climbed

out of bed and went over to my backpack. I took out the picture of my mother and handed it to Viv.

"That's the girl," Viv said, positively.

"No," I said. "That's my mother. That's my mother when she was our age."

Viv looked at the photograph, and then at me, and then at it, and then at me. She frowned. "What? But that girl—Kayla—So what's going on? You were separated at birth? She's your long-lost twin?"

"No," I said. "Close, but no. Actually, I've been thinking that the best word for our relationship is probably littermates. Although it's far from exact."

And as Viv stared, I began pacing again. "Okay, listen. It'll sound like science fiction, but it turns out that my mother went to Dr. Wyatt twenty years ago looking for a way to have a child who definitely wouldn't have HD. She took fertility drugs and produced a bunch of eggs and the eggs were fertilized in vitro.

"It was all definitely, uh, irregular, but it happened. Dr. Wyatt checked the embryos that survived and that divided normally for the HD gene sequence. And well, in short—I came from one of those embryos and Kayla came from another."

I didn't look at Viv, but I could feel her astonishment. "Kayla was born before me. Almost a year earlier. I don't really understand how that happened. Well, I guess they froze me for a while. You can freeze a fertilized egg. I understand the how of that, just not the why."

"There was a surrogate mother who carried Kayla to term?" Viv's voice was very faint. "Not your mother?"

I discovered that I could look at Viv again. She was sitting on the edge of the bed, legs dangling, watching me. "Yeah," I said. "I guess. I don't know what happened with Kayla except what I already told you. I walked out on Dr. Wyatt today, after he told me as much as I've just said. I couldn't hear any more.

"And I haven't talked to my father, haven't asked him anything. I know I ought to. I just can't. I do know he hates Dr. Wyatt, but he's been refusing to tell me why. He says he's thinking about telling me, but he hasn't. It has to have something to do with all this, though. It has to. And now—I don't know, Viv. I don't want to push him. I'm not even sure I want to know anything more. It's all—I don't know. I don't know."

A long silence. Then: "Well," Viv said, finally. "It's a lot to take in. It does sound incredible, Eli. My head is reeling."

"I'm telling the truth." It came out defensively, angrily.

Viv stood up and walked over to me. "I believe you." She kissed me. Then she turned and began to get dressed.

"Viv?" I was incredulous. "You're leaving?"

"No." She turned, and there was a look on her face I had seen before—in the bathroom in the fifth grade, when she'd set out to protect Asa Barnes. Mingled fear and determination. "Eli, we have to wake up your father so you can talk to him."

"No," I said. "I'm not ready yet."

"I don't care," Viv said quietly. "I am going to make you."

"You can't." Panic pushed at me.

"Watch me," said Viv, and walked right out of my room.

CHAPTER 33

I TRAILED VIV INTO THE HALLWAY, watching with disbelief as she flicked on the light and rapped at my father's bedroom door. "Mr. Samuels? It's Vivian." When at first there was no reply, she took in a deep breath and began pounding. "Mr. Samuels! Please wake up. It's not an emergency, but it's important!"

My panic was replaced by blind terror. I backed into my room, snatched up a pair of jeans and a T-shirt, and was dressed in ten seconds. I pushed my feet into sneakers. I was in the hallway again just as my father, in a robe, opened his door.

"Is everything all right?"

I didn't pause to listen to Viv explain. I shoved past them both. I had my hand on the doorknob when I felt Viv's full weight land on my back. "No!" she yelled. "Eli, don't you dare run away! You coward!" Her arms were around my shoulders, clutching. Her knees gripped my hips.

It was true. I was a coward. And I knew exactly what I was afraid of.

I was afraid to discover that my father might not be my father. That the experiment involving my conception had indeed involved chimeralike activities with my DNA, activities that split my parentage in strange, untraceable ways. And that my father knew . . . and that this was the source of his hatred for Dr. Wyatt. And that this was why he was reluctant to tell me.

I knew my father loved me. Even if I were some unnatural mishmash of DNA—even if I were not his, or not fully his—he loved me. But . . . but this—did adopted children feel like this? Or was this some strange new, unhuman emotion?

"I'm sorry," Viv was saying. She slid down from my back but kept one hand firmly on my arm. "But the two of you have to talk. Mr. Samuels, Eli knows stuff—and you know stuff . . . this is about Dr. Wyatt, of course—you have to tell each other . . . Eli's scared, Mr. Samuels, you have to—"

My father cut her off. "I agree," he said calmly.

"Oh," said Viv uncertainly. "But—Eli? If your father will talk to you, will you talk to him? Eli?"

I didn't answer. I slumped against the wall.

"Eli?"

Finally I nodded.

The sequence of events after that was a little unclear to me, but somehow my father got dressed and the three of us drove to Viv's apartment and dropped her off. Then it was my father and me, alone in his old silver Toyota Camry at four in the morning. My father drove a short distance to the library lot and parked there, leaving the motor running. I felt the enclosed space of the car press in around us. I was glad that it was still dark.

"Don't be angry at Viv," my father said. "She did the right thing. I've left this too long already."

I said, "She shouldn't have forced things."

My father spoke quietly, without moving his eyes from the steering wheel. "It was you who forced things. You made the decision weeks ago to pursue this." An edge of impatience crept into his voice. "You didn't stumble onto Dr. Wyatt. You went looking for him. I tried to stop you, but you wouldn't stop."

I drew in a breath. "I'm sorry."

There was a moment of silence, and then my father reached out and covered my hand with his. "It's okay."

"You were right to try to stop me," I blurted.

"No. Now I think I was wrong not to tell you long ago."

That shut me up.

He returned his hand to the steering wheel and added: "But that doesn't matter now. What matters is that you know how much I love you. How proud I am of you."

I had known he would say that. I knew that he felt it. But still, still, it was good to hear.

"I do know," I said. We sat another moment. Then I said, "Okay. Are you ready now?"

"Yes."

Now it was my turn to look straight ahead while I spoke. "I already know what Dr. Wyatt told me about my conception— that Mom wanted to be sure she wouldn't have a baby with HD, and he decided to help. That he gave her hormones to produce eggs, and then he examined all the eggs to search for one without HD."

"Yes." My father seemed to be choosing his words carefully. "Originally, I thought we should just not have children. Not take any risk. But your mother was determined. She was functioning from desperation, and Wyatt—to be honest, I thought he had to be both immoral and a crackpot to come up with this plan. But your mother begged me. And despite all my doubts—I couldn't say no. I let myself be persuaded."

He looked at me intently then. "And I will never be sorry that you exist. Never. Even if you did have HD—and you don't, we accomplished that—I would not be sorry."

"But then why do you hate Dr. Wyatt?" I asked. "Why aren't you grateful? Mom was grateful, wasn't she?"

"Yes," said my father. "She was."

"Then—"

"Eli," said my father quietly, "have you ever heard the saying about nothing coming without a price?"

"Of course."

"There was a price for you, Eli, and your mother agreed to pay it without consulting me. I suppose that was her right. But I don't have to like it, and I never will."

I thought I knew. But I asked anyway. "What was the price, Dad?"

He turned and looked at me, even though, in the dark, I couldn't see his expression. "The other eggs. Wyatt got all of your mother's extra eggs to keep."

My stomach convulsed.

Kayla.

"I didn't know at first." There was a pleading note in my father's voice. "I swear to you, Eli, I didn't know about that part of the bargain until after Ava was pregnant with you and Wyatt had assured us that you did not have HD. Ava knew I'd have a problem with their agreement. She told me it was her business, hers and Wyatt's. Her body, her choice. Not mine. I was only involved in your conception."

"Dad . . ."

"But I dream about them," my father said starkly. "I feel that they . . . wherever they are, maybe still in embryo, frozen— that they are my children somehow. Not genetically, I know that. But my responsibility. And I've failed them, because . . . because he's not a man you would trust with a child. I knew that the minute I met him. Brilliant, yes. But that's not important. At least, I don't think it is."

He swallowed. "Eli, we let him have the eggs. We gave him dozens of potential children to play with, in exchange for you."

CHAPTER 34

LATER THAT MORNING, my father drove me to work. He'd asked me if I wanted to take another day off and spend it with him, talking, but I said no. I think we were both a little relieved. It wasn't that there was no more to say between us. It was that there was almost too much.

I had said to him, "But Kayla's okay." I had not had to say more. He knew exactly who I meant. Of course, he had known who Kayla must be when he saw her at the memorial service; when he gave me my mother's picture. "Kayla's okay," I said. "I know her; I tell you, she's fine. Or at least she's as okay as I am."

My father hesitated. "I suppose." There was a note of doubt in his voice that puzzled me. "But what about the others?" he went on. "If there are any others?"

I had not had an answer. My stomach had roiled again. My father thought Dr. Wyatt was unethical. But there wasn't evidence of that, was there? I was fine. Kayla was fine. Others—if there were others . . . conceived in vitro, born to surrogate parents . . . why wouldn't they be fine, too? He was a genius, even my father had had to concede that.

Waste products.

"We'll talk more later," I had said to my father.

But now, as I stood in front of the Wyatt Transgenics building and watched him drive off, returning to the packing up of all the bits and pieces of my mother's final life, I was filled with so much sadness and fear that I had to turn abruptly away. I wanted to bawl like a child that I needed him and he ought to know better, even if I didn't, than to leave me alone, alone with the weight of what I now knew. But I breathed in and out and then it was over. I wasn't a child. I wouldn't let myself feel or act like one.

I went into the building.

Even though to me it felt as if I were late, I was the first one in my lab. I ignored my work for just a few more minutes and called Viv. I told her I had had a good talk with my father and would see her later. Then I sat at my computer and addressed the things I was supposed to do, as if nothing had happened.

It felt surprisingly good to work, and as the day passed and I ticked one item after another off my task list, I was actually able to forget for short periods of time. I found an interesting anomaly in the data for the current experiment—were the does producing a little too much protein in their milk?—and pointed it out to Larry, who clapped me on the shoulder and said it was good to have me back.

Then all at once it was after six o'clock and the last of

my colleagues were leaving. Larry called back to me: "Go home, Eli!"

"I will!" I yelled, but the thick lab door had already closed and I wasn't sure if he'd heard me . . . well . . .

If he'd heard me lie. Because I wasn't going home. Not yet, anyway. I was supposed to meet Viv at my apartment at 8:30, and I had plans for between now and then. They had been percolating on a subconscious level all day.

I logged off my computer and shut it down. I wandered into the rabbits' room and found myself in front of Foo-foo's cage.

"Foo," I said softly. "Mind if I run something by you?"

Foo-foo's ears moved as I spoke, which was enough agreement for me.

"Dr. Wyatt told me that my mother's request changed the course of his intellectual life. But we don't work with human fertility and human genetic manipulation here at Wyatt Transgenics. We develop protein enzymes in animal milk. And now I know about all those other human eggs . . . my mother's . . ." I paused. I said, "Foo? Remember that little elevator?"

Foo-foo's whiskers twitched.

"Oh, don't worry," I said. "I'm going alone this time." Although, as I spoke, I found myself wondering if it really would be such a bad idea to bring Foo-foo. Of course, I'd get in trouble if anyone saw us. But then again, if I did get caught, wouldn't I look more innocent if Foo-foo—rather than, say, my father or Viv—was with me? I could even say I'd been chasing her again.

I unlatched Foo-foo's cage and tucked her into my arms.

Then, faster than Foo-foo herself could have hopped it, we were on our way.

It's not uncommon for scientists to work odd hours, so it was very possible that I'd encounter someone who'd stayed late. But as I strode through the corridors toward the little dead-end hallway with its mysterious elevator, I didn't feel furtive. And my luck held: I met no one until I crossed the bridge above the mezzanine. There, however, I somehow caught the eye of the security guard sitting below the double-helix staircase at the reception desk.

But it was fine. Keeping a firm hold on Foo-foo, I waved confidently at the guard and kept walking—and he waved back and returned to working his crossword puzzle.

Finally, we arrived in the darkened Human Resources area, in the hallway facing the closed "utility room." I fitted my access card into the slot and pulled the concealing door open. Then I stepped into the empty elevator and tried the key there as well, sliding it into the mechanism and pressing the button for the lower basement.

Nothing happened. I leaned toward the control panel with concentration. I tried all sorts of different combinations, swiping the card first and pushing a button, and then the reverse. I even tried rubbing Foo-foo's foot, for good luck. But the elevator doors stayed stubbornly open, and its panel buttons remained unlit.

I would have to give up, at least for now. Still . . .

"Listen, little rabbit Foo-foo," I said. "There have to be stairs somewhere. Maybe I can find them if I study the plans Viv copied. We could try breaking in that way tomorrow."

Foo-foo didn't say anything. But someone else did, from behind me.

"Eli?" The voice was pitched high with astonishment. Foo-foo twitched strongly in my arms. But I had a firm grip, and after a couple of seconds, she subsided.

I knew who it was. What I didn't know was whether I was ready to cope. But there was no choice. I turned.

Kayla Matheson was standing just outside the elevator, beautiful in white jeans and a black tank top. She looked at me and then at Foo-foo, and her mouth dropped open and stayed there.

My heart was pounding now. I knew Foo-foo could feel it, and that it might alarm her, so I tucked my other arm around her and held her closely, warmly.

Questions—*What are you doing here? Where's Dr. Wyatt? Are you going to tell on me?*—flashed through my mind but then were gone, leaving behind the only real questions, the essential questions.

Do you know about us? About you and me and how we came into this world? Do you know about my—our—mother?

I realized that Kayla must have overheard what I'd said to Foo-foo about breaking in, but at that moment it didn't matter at all.

Once I got it working, my voice came out a little croaky. "Kayla, this is my pal Foo-foo Fourteen. Foo-foo, this is Kayla."

My sister.

I didn't say it, but I felt it. I felt it in the air between Kayla and me. Could she feel it, too? I didn't know; couldn't tell.

Kayla seemed to have recovered from her surprise at seeing

Foo-foo. "Am I wrong, Eli, or did you just say you wanted to break into the subbasement?" She didn't look shocked or even disapproving.

"Yes," I said.

She was silent for just long enough to make me think she wasn't going to say anything more. Then the strangest little smile distorted one corner of her mouth. "Funny. I was just going to try that myself."

And as astonishment filled me, Kayla held out one hand, and I saw that she was clutching a card key. "This one ought to work," she said. "Because I stole it from Quincy this morning."

CHAPTER 35

"IT'LL PROBABLY WORK, THEN," I managed.

Kayla stepped inside the elevator. "He thinks he mislaid it," she said conversationally. She swiped the card into the slot on the control panel and the panel came alive instantly. The doors slid shut but the elevator remained stationary.

Kayla reached past me and stabbed at the B5 button with her index finger. The elevator began to sink downward. "I have a very specific errand in the subbasement. In fact—" She glanced at me swiftly, half-questioningly. "I'm wondering if you might be a big help. You know a lot about databases, don't you?"

She had an errand involving computer databases? One she'd needed to steal the access key to accomplish? I was wary. No matter what Dr. Wyatt was up to, it would be a serious, almost evil, act for me to alter or destroy clinical data. That had been drummed into me. But maybe Kayla only wanted to look at something. That was different. Actually, whatever this data was, I wanted to examine it, too. Oh, yes, I did.

And if she believed there was data in subbasement 5, then maybe there wasn't anything—anybody—else down there. Data. I could live with data. I'd be delighted to find data.

"I'm happy to see what I can do for you," I temporized, adding, "I'm guessing you've been in the subbasement before? You know what's there?"

"Oh, yeah. I got the official tour from Quincy last week." Was there a bitter note in her voice? "What about you? When was your tour? And what's your agenda today? Obviously, it's covert, but you can tell me."

I looked at Kayla. "Actually, I haven't had any tour, official or otherwise. And my agenda was just to look around. Covertly, I guess. So, what's down here, anyway?"

Kayla gasped. "You mean you don't—" The elevator came to a stop and its door began to open. But Kayla slammed her hand onto the button that closed it again and stood so that her body blocked the control panel.

"Sorry, Eli," she said quietly. "In deciding to take you down here, I made an assumption I shouldn't have made."

"What—" I began.

"How much do you know?" she cut in. Her eyes locked on mine and they went a little . . . well, desperate.

I never had a thought of not telling her, but I found I could not watch her while I did. I stepped back and leaned against the opposite wall of the elevator. I held the quivering Foo-foo in my arms, and I looked down at the rabbit and stroked her while I talked.

It gave us both some privacy.

I told Kayla that I had only recently learned that Dr. Wyatt had assisted my mother in having a child without HD, and that I suspected he had also made some genetic-level changes to me. I told her about my Alice-in-Wonderland chase of Foo-foo to this hidden elevator.

Then I told her that she was my mother's child as well. I told her that my mother had given Dr. Wyatt her extra eggs; that this had been Dr. Wyatt's price for helping her—and that my mother had paid it without concern. I said that I had not known—still did not know—how to assimilate that information.

It didn't actually take me very long to tell her all this.

When I had finished, I raised my eyes and found that the desperation had seeped out of Kayla's. She just looked tired. I hesitated, and then asked: "Have I told you anything you didn't already know?"

She nodded. "I didn't know who she was," she said simply, and I knew she meant my—our—mother. "I knew what had happened, scientifically, before my birth; my parents told me a long time ago that there had been a donor egg—though my father seems to feel he is my genetic father. But I didn't know my mother's name or anything about her, and neither did my parents. That was one of the things I thought I would find out today. I was going to look for it in Quincy's files. I never imagined . . ." Her voice trailed off.

I couldn't think of anything to say. I wondered why Dr. Wyatt hadn't told Kayla at least some things about my—our—mother, considering that he'd felt comfortable in telling her so much. Comfortable enough to give her a tour of whatever he was doing in the basement. Comfortable enough to introduce her to me. Comfortable enough to tell me.

Strange. But maybe he thought it didn't matter to her? Maybe he'd promised her parents, the Mathesons, not to tell? Or maybe—could he have wanted me to tell her?

Kayla said, "I can hardly believe it. I was at her memorial service."

I pulled my thoughts back to the present. "Yes. You know something? I'm glad you were there."

"Me, too," said Kayla, but her voice was uncertain.

I wanted more than anything to touch her, to hug her. To make contact somehow and let her know . . . something. Let her know I was there. But she was holding herself so straight. So separate. We were strangers.

I blurted, "Would you like to hold the rabbit for a while? She's, um, she's sort of soft and warm."

Kayla looked at Foo-foo warily, but then said, "Oh. Okay."

As gently as if I were transferring an infant into another person's arms, I handed the rabbit over to Kayla. I had to show Kayla how to hold her, but then Foo-foo settled in comfortably against Kayla's breast, her nose pink as pink.

"Huh," said Kayla.

"I'm getting pretty fond of Foo-foo," I confessed.

Was that a trace of a smile on Kayla's face? "I wish I'd seen you chasing her."

"It was surreal," I said.

We watched each other. The atmosphere between us was awkward, but it wasn't unpleasant. It was just . . . new.

"Well," Kayla said, finally. "Let's get out of this elevator now, okay? I'll show you around down here. And I still want to look at Quincy's computer. There're some things . . ."

"I'd appreciate that," I said. "I'm obviously curious to see everything. Including the computer. And you'll tell me what's going on down here?"

"Yes," said Kayla. "What I know. Which is more than you do, but I'm still piecing things together also. Trying to figure out . . . decide . . . well. Just some stuff." A troubled look passed over her face. She moved out of the way of the control panel, and I pressed the button to open the elevator door.

As we emerged, Kayla cuddled Foo-foo a little more closely, and I saw her dip her head to brush her cheek against the rabbit's warm, soft back.

CHAPTER 36

WE STOOD TOGETHER in a very small utilitarian hallway, and I instantly realized that this basement area must not stretch the full length and width of the building and basement levels above. In the hallway, we were confronted by three closed doors. They had no signs or labels, only numbers. 1. 2. 3.

For some reason, that struck me as funny. "What's behind door number one?" I said.

Kayla wasn't amused—but then, she'd been here before. "That's the apartment. You should look at it, but I don't want to waste much time there. The office is in two, and the exam room and lab in three, and they're more important."

"Just an apartment?" I said. "We can skip it. The lab—"

"No. You ought to see." Kayla was hunching her shoulders. She slipped Dr. Wyatt's card key into the slot next to the first door and put her hand on the knob, turning it when the mechanism unlocked the door.

"Want me to take the rabbit?" I asked.

"No." She had both arms cradling Foo-foo again. She used her hip to nudge the door open and jerked her chin for me to follow her inside. I did.

We had entered the living/dining area of a furnished apartment. There was plush off-white wall-to-wall carpet on the floor, and pale yellow paint on the walls. A sofa, love seat, and chair upholstered in denim were clustered around an oak coffee table in the living room area. Beyond them was a small oak dining table and chairs. Next to that, beyond a pass-through window, there was a kitchen with stainless steel appliances. On the walls hung framed art prints: the Picasso drawing of a hand holding flowers; "Doors of Boston"; a 1920's poster reproduction advertising a cruise.

It was a pleasant, neutral living space, with one anomaly: There were clear signs that one or more small children were expected and welcome. A tall bookshelf against one of the walls in the living room held bright red and yellow plastic containers of toys as well as a large collection of picture books. I spotted a rubber duck, a teddy bear, and a doll dressed like a pioneer girl. Lastly, beside the bookcase stood an enormous canister of Tinkertoys, which made me remember my first meeting with Dr. Wyatt.

Without speaking, Kayla and I prowled, discovering a bathroom and two bedrooms. The first bedroom had a queen-sized bed, but the second was again furnished for young children, with sturdy bunk beds and more shelves of toys and games and books. A crib and bassinet stood in one corner. On the walls were children's posters: Mickey Mouse and Oscar the Grouch and Sailor Moon and Barney.

I looked at it all and knew that what my father had feared was true.

Kayla was watching me.

My voice was level when I spoke. "He made more of us, didn't he? More children like you and me. My—our—mother's children."

"Yes," said Kayla. "There are a few others now. Three toddlers. One baby."

I had thought I was ready to hear it, but I wasn't. I turned abruptly and left the room. When I reached the living room, I found I had to sit down. I did, on the sofa.

They must all be chimeras, I thought. That would have been the scientific lure that tempted Dr. Wyatt. He'd wanted to see if he could use transgenic technology successfully in humans. And Kayla, too, must be a chimera. My "dry run" theory no longer had much credibility. At least, I didn't believe in it.

Kayla had followed me to the living room. "Listen," she said. "For the longest time, it was just me—um, and you. But then Quincy built this place. He told me the other day, when he showed it to me, that scientific techniques had improved. He had more certainty of success now, and so it was finally time. Before, he didn't want to waste any of the—the material. The eggs. I guess he'd tried before, after you and me, and it didn't go well. He lost several . . . Well, he lost several."

I was watching her, but I wasn't really seeing her. I was seeing Dr. Wyatt.

"He told me I was a miracle," Kayla said. "A one-in-a-million. Beginner's luck."

Her voice was impassive. I couldn't tell what she thought.

"Four new children," I finally said. "And they visit this place for—for what?"

"Quincy has a whole battery of tests and evaluations, both physical and psychological. They take several days to run through, because he doesn't want the—the subject to be too stressed or anxious, and it's best if it feels like a game. The environment should be as calm and controlled as possible—relaxing, homelike. Private, of course. With a nice calming adult nearby. The mother, if possible."

"The mother," I repeated.

"The adoptive mother," Kayla clarified, unnecessarily.

"Why does he test the—the children?" I asked. I was breathing more easily.

"They're just development tests. Intensive, but nothing really weird." Was Kayla's gaze sharper now, as it rested on me? "Actually, I'm pretty sure you took his adult physical test battery yourself, Eli. The one I've been taking twice a year. He told me that he'd sent you over to Mass General Hospital before you started working here."

I frowned. "Yes . . . Judith Ryan—this woman in Human Resources—told me my employment was conditional upon a full physical exam." And now I remembered telling Viv about the test; remembered her saying, offhandedly, that the garden shop hadn't bothered even to ask her about her health, let alone send her for a physical.

What a fool I had been.

"Quincy was pretty excited," Kayla was saying. "I think he'd considered you to be irretrievable data. At some point—mark my words—he'll approach you about doing the full test suite."

"Kayla," I said. I looked around the apartment and gestured, unable to find words. Confused thoughts about X-Men and Spider-Man and various fictional, genetically mutated or otherwise altered superheroes—and monsters—chased each other through my head. Swampy. Question upon frantic question crowded into my head and then was interrupted by the next one. A lifetime might not be long enough to find all the questions, and to answer them . . . along with the final, the essential question: *Who was I?*

Was I a chimera, too? Or was I merely what my mother had asked for: an ordinary HD-negative human being? I knew the answer. If I had been born before Kayla, there might have still been room for doubt. But I had not been.

I looked up then and realized that Kayla had been watching me.

"I've been tested again and again since before I can remember," she said gently. Carefully.

I still had no words, but I managed to nod.

And Kayla nodded, as well—and I saw, deep in her eyes, the twin of the suppressed fear that I felt. And the same question: *Who am I? What am I?*

Then Kayla swallowed and continued. "I wasn't tested here, though. This place is pretty new—just four years—and I'd never seen it before Quincy showed it to me the other day. My parents and I used to visit Quincy at his country place in Vermont. Uncle Quincy." Was that bitterness in her voice? I couldn't quite tell, and she had lowered her face as she cuddled Foo-foo. "All the tests—I thought we were just playing games. I used to look forward to going."

"Kayla," I said. "Kayla, do you know—" I stopped.

She looked up. "Know what?"

"Know exactly what he did to us?" I said. "What he did to our genetic structure? What was altered or added or changed? And what has he done to—to—" I could hear my father's voice. *My children. My responsibility.*

"—to our sisters or brothers?" I finished.

Kayla shook her head.

I stood up. "Doors two and three. Lab and office. I bet it's all in there. And that's really where you were headed, isn't it?"

"Yes."

"Let's go," I said. And privately, I thought: I'll find out about the others, Dad. I promise.

CHAPTER 37

WE PASSED QUICKLY through the exam rooms and lab, though if I hadn't felt the pressure of time, I would have wanted to linger and pay more attention. There were two replicas of a standard doctor's examination room. There was a spacious, pristine laboratory, with stainless steel refrigerators, a locking walk-in freezer, and a hooded working area with state-of-the-art equipment.

I felt my steps slow as I looked at the freezer. I wondered if my mother's eggs were in there . . . and if any other woman's were now, too. Fertilized. Unfertilized. Normal or altered DNA. Any eggs would be carefully labeled, I knew. Eggs, sperm, embryos . . . human genetic material. So fragile. So easily destroyed. Nobody could stop me, not if I were determined. Kayla couldn't, even if she wanted to.

Would it be the right thing to do, though? Confusion filled me. *Thou shalt not kill.* But the Ten Commandments didn't specify *Thou shalt not create.* I had been assuming that all this was bad—because, I realized, everything about my father's attitude had told me that it was.

But—was it? Was it really? Was it so wrong that Kayla was alive? That I was?

Maybe I'd seen too many evil scientist movies. Maybe I was jumping to irrational, emotional conclusions. This was Dr. Quincy Wyatt, after all. One of the greatest minds of our time. Who was my father—an ordinary, beaten-down, nearly penniless psychotherapist—to second-guess him? Who was I?

And the destruction of a few eggs—what would that really mean? It wouldn't destroy the underlying knowledge. Or the fact that what Dr. Wyatt was doing was—it had to be—inevitable. It was the next step in human development: taking control of our own destiny ourselves. If it wasn't Dr. Wyatt who led the way now, then it would be someone else, soon.

We humans *are* going to tinker with our genetic makeup. The human genome is a locked box that we are going to pry open. Any mistakes, missteps, problems, unanticipated difficulties—they will be the inevitable price of progress, the price of the good that will surely result as well. Cures for disease; an end to suffering like my mother's. Who knows what? But good stuff. Good stuff.

Surely, good stuff?

"Come on, Eli," Kayla said impatiently. "The computers are through here, and that's where all the information has got to be."

Brought back from my thoughts, I turned to her. I could see her increased tension in the tautness of her arms as they held Foo-foo.

"Okay," I said. I increased the length of my stride to keep pace with her, and so only caught a glimpse, as we passed, of a carpeted exercise room that held top-of-the-line rowing machines and treadmills and stair climbers and stationary bicycles. It was only after we'd moved on that I realized what had been so strange about it.

All of the exercise machines were in miniature.

With that, I refocused. The children. What I really wanted was some information about the children, for my father. For me. Maybe just names and addresses so we could check on them; make sure they were safe. Loved. And—and I wanted my own genetic profile; I wanted the report of what Dr. Wyatt had done to me when I was an embryo. The rest—I could, I *would*, sort it all out later.

Kayla had turned the corner into a room that, I knew instantly upon entering, was Dr. Wyatt's office. It was set up exactly like his office upstairs—a narrow shoe box of a room with two folding tables parallel to each other. Books and journals were heaped in piles on the floor. Steel cabinet doors hung ajar, revealing insides that were crammed untidily full of more papers and books, wires, boxes. The office chairs were old and rickety—though not armless. And yes, there were computers. Two of them; and these, at least, were expensive and new. In fact, they practically gleamed.

"Each of us checks one," Kayla ordered. "Just tell me what the scientific data would look like."

"We'll just be looking for notes," I said. "Maybe in ordinary word processing files, maybe in a database file. I'd guess we should scan all files looking for dates beginning twenty years ago, and for our own names, and for other familiar information. Maybe we'll be lucky and he won't have encrypted the data, though that's probably wishful thinking—"

Kayla interrupted me. "Wait a second, Eli, could you empty out that cardboard box for me, please?" With her foot, she indicated a packing box that held an old monitor. "I want to put the rabbit in it."

"Good idea." I pulled the monitor from the box, and Kayla placed Foo-foo inside. The rabbit backed herself up into a corner and deposited a couple of pellets and, in the middle of everything, I was amused. "Sorry, Foo," I found myself saying. "You'll go home soon, I promise."

Kayla asked curiously, "Why'd you bring her, anyway?"

I hesitated, then told the truth. "For comfort." I didn't wait to see Kayla's reaction. I sat down at one of the computers and got busy. After a moment, I heard her do the same.

It wasn't difficult to find what I sought because, apart from programs, the only data on the computer was located in a folder called "AvaSamuels." Beneath it were lots of files and folders, including a great many that began with the letters KM. For Kayla Matheson, I assumed.

And yes—a click on the first few files told me that they were indeed password-protected and encrypted. It was a wonder, in fact, that there hadn't been a password put on the system as a whole.

"I've found stuff," I said tersely to Kayla. Her chair collided with the back of mine as she got up, moving to stand behind me, leaning over my shoulder. I could hear her breathing—it had sped up. I started to use a few simple tricks to guess the password and encryption key that would open the first KM file, the one dated twenty years ago. Tension knotted the air around us as each trick failed. "This is not going to work," I said finally. "And there's too much here for us to read it all now, anyway, even if we did get in."

"Could you email the data to yourself and then we could try to get into it on your computer?" Kayla asked.

"There's no Internet connection on this machine," I said. "No way to transfer data out—or in. Standard security provision—foolproof." I tapped my fingers on the tabletop. "But you're right—if we can make a copy, we can take it with us. He's got to have the means for copying down here somewhere." I stood up and began prowling through the cabinets. Even a set of diskettes would do.

While I searched, Kayla sat down at my machine and began typing on the keyboard.

"We don't want to monkey around too much with those files," I cautioned. "If we enter too many wrong passwords, it might activate a booby-trap that would shut the machine down completely so we can't even make a backup."

"I'm in," said Kayla calmly.

Now it was my turn to rush up behind the computer. She had the first KM file open.

"My birth date was the password," she said. "And the encryption key was my name."

"Oh," I said. "Good work. But we'll still want to back everything up and take it away. It'll take days to read everything."

I stopped talking as what I was seeing on the screen in front of Kayla penetrated. It was a shorthand code listing precisely what the DNA structure was for each chromosome. I could only just barely recognize it, only just begin to decode what it meant, but it was clear what it was: I could see, for example, where chromosome one began and ended.

"Good God," Kayla said. She scrolled the file down, and there was the notation for the second chromosome . . . and the third. Very occasionally, some of the notation was in red, indicating—what? A change? While the black letters were the regular DNA code? And then there were some stretches of black letters with strikethrough. Was that a cut?

Kayla scrolled down further in the file. "Unbelievable. Is this as meaningless to you as it is to me?"

I didn't answer. We had reached chromosome four. The notation for the map of Kayla's chromosome four. For the tip of chromosome four.

C-A-G, it said. *Repeats: 59.*

"Well?" said Kayla impatiently. "Should we try another file and hope for plain English?"

C-A-G. Repeats: 59.

I found that I had grabbed the back of Kayla's chair with both hands. I was gripping it with all my strength. My knuckles were white.

I knew now. I understood why Kayla was older than me. Simply, Kayla's egg had not fit my mother's specifications. It had not been negative for HD. And—whatever else Dr. Wyatt may or may not have been able to do twenty years ago—he had not been capable of trimming the C-A-G repeat down to a safe length.

I had been running from the C-A-G repeat all my life. I had

just been freed from it, finally and definitely. And yet—I swear—if at that moment I could have switched my chromosome four with Kayla's, I would have. I would have.

"Eli?" Kayla said sharply. "What are you seeing? You can read this, can't you? What does it mean? What do you see?"

I found my voice, and—thank God—it came out strong and definite, a bit regretful. "No, sorry," I said to my beautiful sister. "I can't read it. It doesn't make any sense to me at all. It's gibberish."

I thought I would get away with it. Kayla's face was averted. But then she turned so that I couldn't avoid her eyes, and they had that desperate expression again, the one she'd worn in the elevator.

"Don't lie to me, Eli," she said. "Tell me what you see."

CHAPTER 38

Maybe I should have insisted that I wasn't lying. Hundreds of times, I have rethought the decision, the choice, of that instant—an instant that stretched out between Kayla and me until it seemed to fill the childhood we had not had together. An instant that marked the borderline between that nonexistent childhood, and the adulthood that we would indeed share.

If I had continued to lie, it might have made a difference to what happened. Or it might not have. I am still only human. I don't know.

What I did was this. I nodded once, and kept my eyes on hers. Then I said, "Ava Samuels died of Huntington's disease. You know that, right?"

"Yes." Kayla's face was still expressionless.

I reached out with my finger over Kayla's shoulder. I pointed at the screen.

C-A-G. Repeats: 59.

"That's the marker for HD," I said. "On chromosome four."

"This is Ava's genetic profile?" Kayla said. "I know it's my initials on the file, but it's the first file, so he put her DNA code in here first?"

Another chance to lie, but I didn't take it. I said nothing, trying to find the right words, and then, three seconds—an eternity—later, I heard her indrawn breath, and realized that I didn't have to search for those words any longer.

I hadn't thought there could be a worse moment than the one in which I had recognized the code.

"Oh," Kayla said. "I see."

I discovered that I had moved my hands onto her shoulders. I felt them rise and fall, rise and fall. I looked at the screen and I felt that line of code imprint itself on my brain.

When I close my eyes to sleep at night—even when I am holding Viv—I see the code. I will see it all my life.

Kayla spoke again. The only sign of what she'd just learned was in the higher-than-normal timbre of her voice. "Eli, would you please hand me the rabbit?"

I did. I stood there for several minutes, watching the quarter of my sister's face that I could see. Her lashes flickered and fell over her eyes. Her shoulders hunched as she cradled the rabbit.

C-A-G. Repeats: 59.

"You aren't alone, Kayla," I said. "You're not going to be alone with this. I'm your brother, okay? I'm your brother. You have to know that. I need you to know that."

My responsibility. Because I am my father's son. Because I choose, like he did, not to walk away. Because you are more than your genes. Because you are human. Because you are worth it.

She didn't answer. And after a while, without having made a conscious decision to do so, I got to work. I didn't care anymore about leaving the room undisturbed. I dismantled both computers, removing their hard drives, wrapping them in towels from the apartment, and packing them in the cardboard box, using more towels for protective padding. I found a pile of diskettes and CDs in one of the cabinets, noticed that several of the CDs were backups, labeled with the names of the files we'd just been viewing, and placed those in the box as well.

As I finished packing the boxes, I finally felt Kayla watching me again. She said, "We'll find someone to give it all to." She was holding Foo-foo with both arms, huddling over her. "They're evidence, the hard drives. Better than copies. Because someone, somewhere, can stop him. This whole place will be of interest to the police, right? It can't be legal, what he's done. There's got to be a law. He's been so secretive . . . it must be illegal."

Probably—though I wondered if the police would be capable of understanding this, of sorting it all out. FBI, maybe? But I also felt as if it didn't really matter right now. What mattered was getting Kayla out of there. What mattered was getting to my father.

"Come on," I said. I started to lead Kayla back out. But there, again without planning, I took us into the lab instead. I looked at the walk-in freezer. I reached out and gave the door a tug, just to test it. Yes, it was locked; locked the old-fashioned way, requiring a key.

Then I knew what I was about to do. I was going to destroy everything I could before we left. Too bad if it was evidence. Too bad if it would help to convict Dr. Wyatt of whatever laws he might have broken. And—too bad if here was the key to unimaginable scientific advances.

I was going to destroy it anyway.

"Stand back," I said tensely to Kayla. "No, farther away. Over by the wall."

She did as I ordered. I put my left hand flat on the door for balance, put my right hand on the door handle, and jerked the door toward me sharply, twisting it against its hinges.

It sheered neatly off. I turned, carrying the door, and leaned it against the wall.

"How did you know you could do that?" Kayla asked.

I shrugged. I believe the truth was that I could have done it even if I were someone else. Someone ordinary—Larry, say. Or even Viv.

Viv could have done it, too, if she had felt what I felt.

Was this how the superheroes—Batman, Spidey, Swampy—felt? Was their complete competence fueled by rage? And, beneath the rage, despair?

At that moment, I understood about adulthood. It is not about being in charge of your own life. It is not about being in control. It is about being helpless.

And hating it.

No number of scientists and dreamers like Quincy Wyatt—no amount of DNA tinkering—would ever change that final human helplessness. But they thought they would. And, because of that, they could not be stopped.

Should they be? I didn't know. I only felt. I could only do what was before me to do, right now. I did not know if I was doing right or wrong. Killing or preserving. Loving or hating.

I did not care.

"Come watch," I said to Kayla. We entered the freezer, and I checked through its contents, which were as carefully labeled as I'd imagined they would be. A meticulous man where it mattered, was Quincy Wyatt. I gathered up all the packages, the ones that belonged to my mother, and the ones that didn't.

Kayla knew without asking what I was doing. "With the freezer open, won't they all be destroyed anyway as they defrost?"

"This will be faster," I said.

I took the samples to the sink and ran hot water over them. Then I unplugged and emptied the refrigerators. Then—simply because I wanted to—I went through the room, smashing everything in my path.

I felt very calm.

Kayla stood in the doorway, held Foo-foo, and watched.

Finally, I picked up the cardboard box containing the computer data. "Now," I said. "We go home to my dad. He'll know who we ought to give the data to, and who we ought to tell about this place. We'll tell him about the other children. He'll know what to do next. He'll advise us. We're in this together from now on, Kayla. Okay?"

Kayla nodded. She seemed dazed, and I wasn't sure how much she had taken in of what I had just said. The sooner I got her home to my dad, I thought, the better. There was something terrifying about the blankness of her face. About the careful way she was moving, as if she might shatter.

In silence we walked together back down the corridor, and I pressed the button for the elevator. After a minute, it opened smoothly.

And we looked into it at Dr. Wyatt.

CHAPTER 39

DR. WYATT LOOKED BACK OUT at us. Then—incredibly—his face split into a delighted smile.

I felt all my muscles tense, and it took everything I had not to—not to—

"You've seen it all!" he said to me. "Kayla showed you—so, what do you think, Eli? Naughty of you two—I would have liked to give you the tour myself, but that doesn't matter. Now we can really talk. Now you'll understand. I want us to—"

From Kayla burst a sound like nothing I had ever heard in this life. It was a wail—a moan—a shriek. It was one word:

"*Why?*"

I had a bare instant in which to see the expression of amazement and bewilderment that dawned on Dr. Wyatt's face. Kayla didn't wait for a response from him. Without warning, she suddenly flung the rabbit through the air in my direction. Then—in a single blur of motion—she hurled herself forward into the elevator, straight at Dr. Wyatt.

Just as quickly as Kayla moved, so did I, instinctively. I dropped the cardboard box and dove, catching Foo-foo a mere inch before she would have hit the floor and, very likely, broken her delicate back. Aware that I had already, involuntarily, chosen the rabbit over Dr. Wyatt—and that Kayla had known I would—I yelled back over my shoulder, "Kayla, no! Don't hurt him—it'll solve nothing! We'll turn him in, we'll—"

Dr. Wyatt's voice, high and frightened, intertwined with mine: "Kay—" His words were cut off by a noise that was strange to me and yet was unmistakable: the thud of his body smashing into the back wall of the elevator. It was followed immediately by another sound that I'd never have dreamed I'd recognize: the crunch of bone.

I knew she meant to kill him. I shoved the trembling Foo-foo safely aside and scrambled to my feet. Two seconds later I, too, was inside the elevator.

Dr. Wyatt was a small heap in the corner, curled into a fetal position on the floor, one arm positioned as if to protect his head, the other hanging at an unnatural angle. His cane lay abandoned a few inches away from him. He was emitting— not a scream, but a weird keening noise.

Kayla stood above him, heel swinging viciously downward to land a sickening smash that quite audibly shattered his chin. She raised her foot again—

I grabbed her from behind, pinning her arms, and lifted her right off the floor. "That's enough," I panted. I turned, staggering out of the elevator with her, back into the corridor.

I knew I couldn't hold Kayla long. She was fighting—kicking, bucking—but not speaking, instead focusing all her energy

237

on breaking my hold. I concentrated on controlling her. Then her foot hooked snakelike around behind my knee, pulling me off balance. I couldn't have stayed upright even if I'd thought that was a good idea. We tumbled down to the carpet and rolled, landing pressed up against the wall—and it was only by good fortune that I was the one on top.

I used my full weight, my full strength, to try to hold her down. I pinned her legs with mine, her arms with my hands. I yelled, "You can't kill him, Kayla!"

Her eyes caught mine for a moment, and I swear that there was no rationality behind them. She was now the one fueled by rage and righteousness and despair. I could feel her left wrist twisting free—her knee inching up—

And then all at once she collapsed beneath me like a popped balloon. Distrustful, I stared down into her eyes, finding them suddenly again alert and intelligent. "What was that noise?" she hissed into my face.

"What?" I stilled, listening—and then recognized the whir of the elevator's motor. Without my willing it, my muscles slackened for a second.

Kayla shoved me violently off of her and rolled to her feet, hurtling herself back toward the elevator. I turned my head just in time to see the door close an instant before Kayla got there.

Her hand slapped the Up button. "Open, damn you, open!" she yelled. But the elevator, with Dr. Wyatt in it, did not reopen.

I climbed painfully to my feet and watched, with Kayla, as the numerical indicator above the elevator door gave evidence of Dr. Wyatt's escape. Finally, it stopped on the ground floor, and stayed there, even though Kayla pounded and pounded on the button.

"He's locked the elevator upstairs," I said.

Kayla gave me one look. "No kidding," she said. "Your fault."

"I couldn't let you kill him," I said. "It would ruin your life. This isn't so bad—hell, I can just use my cell phone to call for help. Call my dad. The police. Whoever. It's over for him, no matter what. It's over, Kayla." I gestured at the cardboard box that contained the computer hard drives. "We have everything we need to get him, and he knows it."

"Use your cell phone, then," said Kayla. Her voice was weary, hopeless.

"Kayla . . ." I stopped. I didn't know what to say.

She was moving away from me now. She walked steadily back down the corridor to where Foo-foo was cowering against the wall. She picked Foo-foo up. She held her.

"Is the rabbit all right?"

"She's scared," said Kayla. "But she'll be okay."

"What about you?"

Kayla didn't answer. She kept her back to me, and finally— my cell phone didn't work underground, but the phone in the office did—I called my father.

EPILOGUE

I KNOCK ON THE WOODEN DOOR of the office.

"Come in!"

I enter as a small, gray-haired woman looks up from her computer. "I'm Eli Samuels," I say. "Sorry I'm late, Dr. Fukuyama."

Rosemary Fukuyama nods toward the window as she removes her half-glasses and lets them dangle from a chain around her neck. "The blizzard of the decade's beginning out there, so I'm impressed you came at all. Though it certainly helps on this campus that we have the tunnels." Then she takes in the fact that my coat and hat are coated with snow. "I guess you didn't use them to get here from your dorm."

I remove my coat and hang it up, then, at her invitation, sit down on the other side of her crowded but tidy desk. "I don't live on the MIT campus, Dr. Fukuyama. I live with my father over near Central Square."

"That's a little unusual." Dr. Fukuyama raises an eyebrow. "Most freshmen want to move away from their families."

I shrug. "There wasn't dorm space for me, even if I'd wanted to live on campus." Which I hadn't; I'd wanted to stay with my father this year at least. "I wasn't originally going to be in this class at all," I tell her. "I applied and was admitted at the last minute, in August, on an exception basis."

"I know." Dr. Fukuyama waves a hand toward her computer. "I was just reading your file. I was particularly intrigued by the letter from Larry Donohue. He was a student of mine."

"Yes," I say. "He was the one who told me to move heaven and earth to try to get into your seminar this semester. He told me he'd email you about it."

Her eyes are intent on me now. "I wouldn't have seen you at all otherwise. My bioethics seminar is exclusively for seniors and graduate students, and I can only admit eight students."

"I want to be one of them," I say. It's only half the truth. What I most want is to know Dr. Rosemary Fukuyama, whose three books on bioethics my father, Viv, Kayla, and I have all read. And, through her, to meet other scientists like her.

"You worked for Larry last summer at General Transgenics?" says Dr. Fukuyama. Her voice lingers an extra moment on the new name of the company. "Tell me about that."

So I tell her about the transgenic rabbits, and the proteins expressed in milk, and my ordinary duties around the lab. But I have the impression that she is only listening on the surface; that she—like most people in biogenetics this past year—can't think of General Transgenics without compulsively wondering about Dr. Wyatt and the incidents of last spring.

Wyatt Transgenics is dead, of course, but General Transgenics lives on without Dr. Wyatt. He disappeared along with

Judith Ryan and three high-ranking scientists on the day that Kayla attacked him in the elevator. Things moved rapidly after that. The federal authorities arrived, the board of directors met, and three days later, the company was reorganized, with a businessman who had a stellar background in the pharmaceutical industry appointed as the new CEO.

Of course, rumors spread like fire around the building and the industry. One popular guess about Dr. Wyatt and the others was that they had participated in an illegal experiment involving human cloning. Even more popular was a theory that they'd embezzled company funds. Indeed, in the weeks that followed the reorganization, accountants swarmed the building like insects. But in the end, the cover-up—or whatever it was—was too tight for anyone to be certain about anything. And, perhaps strangely, and certainly unlike many other major business scandals, there were no public charges filed.

I had no inside information, either, although the federal authorities talked to me and Kayla, a little bit, at the start of the investigation. It had begun with us, after all; begun with my father calling the police after I telephoned him from the sub-basement. But soon enough, the authorities had nothing more to say to us. "We'll handle this," we were told by an impassive, skinny bald man in a blue suit. "It's our job, not yours. Go back to your lives."

So we were left with more unknowns than we could count.

Dr. Fukuyama leans forward. It's become almost standard small talk in the biotech industry to speculate about Dr. Wyatt's whereabouts, so I'm not surprised when she says, "Do you have a theory about where Wyatt is and what he's up to?"

I frame a careful reply. "They told us at General Transgenics that he'd been tracked to Europe before the authorities lost sight of him." I pause and then add, "I wonder if he might have set up a lab in another country."

There are many places in this world, my father says, in which a moneyed scientist can do whatever work he wants, without government oversight, without ethical guidelines, and even, in some cases, with government approval. There are countries where Dr. Wyatt and his research will be welcome. It might even be that his research is actually welcome here, in the U.S. . . . covertly.

"And what do you think Wyatt's doing?" asks Dr. Fukuyama.

"Presumably, whatever it was he was doing at Wyatt Transgenics before he ran," I say.

"Do you subscribe to the theory he's involved in human cloning?"

I shake my head. "No," I say. "That wouldn't be my guess. His primary interest was always transgenics."

She nods. "I agree." Abruptly, she pushes back her chair and turns to stare through the window at the blizzard. I watch her profile. We are quiet for a while, and then she says, "We are standing at a crossroads. At least, I hope we are. I hope we haven't already gone past it while we—as a society, I mean— weren't paying enough attention." She pauses for a second and then says, "Mr. Samuels, I want to tell you a story." She turns back to face me.

She pulls up to her desk again. "Many years ago, I was at a national conference on biogenetics. It wasn't purely a scientific conference; it was open to the public. The idea was that people from all walks of life—intelligent, thoughtful people—would discuss our dreams about what this technology might do for us. There were panel discussions on the eradication of MS, and Parkinson's, and Lou Gehrig's disease, and on and on. We'd identify the genetic flaws, and no one would suffer from them ever again.

"It was tremendously exciting, because there was a feeling that we really would have the potential to eradicate all human suffering from the earth. There was a feeling almost of becoming godlike. It was electrifying, Mr. Samuels.

"I was as exhilarated as anyone. But then, on the last day of the conference, a young man stood up in the audience. We had all been listening to a speech about how prenatal testing was showing promising signs of making it possible to eliminate Down syndrome. And . . ." Dr. Fukuyama leans across the desk, her eyes intent on mine. "Mr. Samuels, the young man who stood up in the audience to talk had Down syndrome himself. He was the head of a self-advocacy group of adults with Down syndrome."

I nod.

"We were all a little taken aback," says Dr. Fukuyama. "But this young man stood up, Mr. Samuels, and he said the following. I have never forgotten it.

" 'I don't understand. We don't make any trouble. We don't steal things or kill people. We don't take the good jobs. Why do you want to kill us?' "

For a few seconds I cannot breathe. I stare at Dr. Fukuyama. She stares back at me. Then she smiles, a little sadly. "That moment changed everything for me. My excitement disappeared. I got a glimpse of the world we really might create, with our high-flying ideas about the eradication of suffering. A world in which so many people are found lacking. Are considered unfit even to be born."

My mother, I think. Kayla.

"There's a difference," Dr. Fukuyama says softly. "That is my point, Mr. Samuels. There's a difference between using gene therapy for the treatment of existing medical conditions, and using our growing, but far from perfect, knowledge of genes—or of humanity—to declare that we absolutely know who has—and who hasn't—a right to life at all."

How a couple chooses to go about having a baby—or indeed, in the future, the genetic makeup of that baby—should be entirely their own business and their own choice.

I lean closer to Dr. Fukuyama. "I don't trust us," I say. My voice cracks. "I don't trust us to be able to decide. Even with the best of intentions—we might think we're eradicating suffering, but are we? We're only human—we don't know what'll happen even tomorrow. How can we make decisions that will affect all our descendants forever? How can we possibly know what's best?" I am clenching my hands in my lap.

Dr. Fukuyama and I look at each other for a moment in silence. Then she says, "I think you should take my seminar, Mr. Samuels. Come to the first class, next Monday at three o'clock."

I nod. I loosen my fists and breathe. "Thank you," I say. I collect my coat and prepare to go. But then, at the door, I turn back. "Dr. Fukuyama?" Suddenly my voice is okay again.

"Yes?"

"This stuff you're talking about—it shouldn't be discussed

only in small groups of graduate students. Exclusivity amounts to secrecy, and I think it's a mistake. It should be discussed everywhere. With everyone. Especially with kids. We ought to try harder to make that happen. *You* ought to."

Dr. Fukuyama's eyes flicker in surprise. I leave.

Outside, the weather is worsening, the wind picking up, the snow falling thick and wet. I trudge back through the storm toward our apartment. I wonder if the weather will keep Viv from coming over for dinner tonight. I wonder what Kayla is doing right now. I think about Dr. Fukuyama's story about the conference and the young man with Down syndrome.

And I wonder what Dr. Fukuyama would think if she could read Dr. Wyatt's research notes about Kayla.

Kayla and I read the notes together, in silence, a couple of days after our time in the subbasement. Even though Dr. Wyatt's hard drives had been taken away by the federal authorities, we had one of the backup CDs, and so we were able to find the answer to the question that Kayla had flung at Dr. Wyatt in the elevator:

Why?

This is what the notes said:

Like its siblings from this first harvest, egg #5 carries the marker for Huntington's disease. However, it is otherwise healthy and will make a good candidate for the experimental gene splicing technique. I will fertilize #5 and then make three carefully selected localized changes to the developing embryo, attempting to encourage superior brain functionality and physical health. While it is unlikely that #5 will survive long enough for implan-

tation in the surrogate, it will nonetheless be useful to see how long it does last, and what effect (if any) my changes have.

This is of course little more than a stab in the dark. I wish I had enough eggs to make only one change at a time; three alterations done together is terrible science. But I don't have material to spare, and I must take the risk. I will remember that every time I lose an egg, I also learn.

Maybe someday, I think, I will show the notes to Dr. Fukuyama. Maybe she will be the one to help us find the words to describe how it felt to read them.

Right now, I don't have those words, and neither does Kayla.

But we do have the data. We have each other. We have two healthy little sisters, in Chicago and in Edgecomb, Maine. And, in Clearwater, Florida, and in Los Angeles, we have one little brother, and one infant sister, who have all sorts of problems.

It's a funny thing. Kayla doesn't discuss her situation with me. But she'll talk about the kids. I think the kids—getting to know them, understanding that they will need her—are what keeps her from despair right now. In time, I must believe, there will be other reasons. Maybe medical reasons. Or maybe just life reasons.

"And it's not like there isn't medical hope," Viv says. "It's not like scientific advancements are *all* suspect or evil. Far from it."

She's right, of course. There is ongoing work in gene therapy. There might be a way, one day, to instruct the extra C-A-G repeats on chromosome four to lie quiet. I pray there will be. It is one of the areas I am determined to study myself. That, at least, is in my control. So much is not.

But—we do have Dr. Wyatt's data. I stole one of the backup CDs before the police arrived in the subbasement, and simply walked out, cradling a thoroughly freaked-out Foo-foo, with the CD hidden securely beneath her bottom.

We have the data, then, and I will learn how to read it and I will learn what it means. Chromosome by chromosome, gene by gene, I will learn who and what we are. But no matter what I learn, no matter what the gene map says, I don't believe it predetermines who we—who anyone—can be. I don't believe it.

I have only to look at my father, after all. We don't know the exact nature of our genetic relationship, my father and I—or even if there is one. We don't know the extent of Wyatt's tinkering with me. But that most profoundly does not matter. Jonathan Samuels is my father. I am his son.

We chose.

I fight my way through the snow and the wind and then I am home.

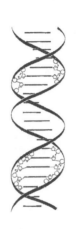

ACKNOWLEDGMENTS

Certainly, I write alone, but on the other hand, I have good company the whole way, and this is where I get to tell those companions how grateful I am for their presence in my life and in my work.

For their careful reading and critique of the entire first draft, my warmest thanks go to Melissa Wyatt, A. M. Jenkins, Anita Riggio, Pat Lowery Collins, and Ellen Wittlinger.

Toni Buzzeo, Jennifer Jacobson, and Franny Billingsley taught me to have faith in reading aloud again. I am in particular grateful to them for encouraging me to read the last chapter of *Double Helix*. "This is a structural mess, and I don't have a clue how to make it work," I said, when I finished reading, and Toni replied, "Don't worry, I do." Toni's, Jennifer's, and Franny's discussion of and then emailed notes on that last chapter were invaluable to me.

I am grateful to Don and Charlene Schuman of Cod Cove Farm Bed & Breakfast in Edgecomb, Maine, where I officially both began and finished this book. Don and Charley create an atmosphere that I can only describe as magical. I am grateful also to my fellow writing retreaters at Cod Cove Farm (the aforementioned Toni, Jennifer, and Franny, along with Deborah Wiles, Jacqueline Briggs-Martin, Jane Kurtz, Joanne Stanbridge, and Dian Curtis Regan). I'm not sure I would have had the courage to begin this book at all—I'd been stalling for months—if I hadn't been able to do it in their company.

I feel great relief as well as gratitude in thanking Dr. Curtis Deutsch, of the Shriver Center at the University of Massachusetts Medical School, for reading my final draft with an eye toward scientific accuracy. I was pretty much on tenterhooks until I heard from him.

With each book, it gets harder and harder to find adequate words for my gratitude to my longtime editor, Lauri Hornik at Dial Books for Young Readers. She remains my most important creative and business partner, from initial idea through final draft.

Finally, I would never even have attempted this book were it not for Conrad O'Donnell, who discussed the current state of genetic research and its implications with me, who chose and hauled in dozens of books for me to read, and who never tired of talking about the story as it unfolded. I share Conrad's unshakeable belief in the equality of all human life.

Thank you all.